THE SECRET OF THE STONE FROG

A TOON GRAPHIC NOVEL BY

DAVID NYTRA

TOON BOOKS IS AN IMPRINT OF CANDLEWICK PRESS

For Mama and Papa

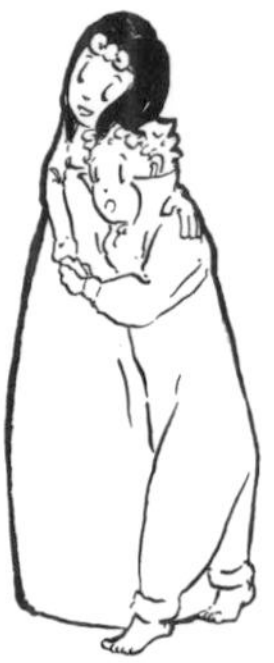

Editorial Director: FRANÇOISE MOULY

Guest Editors: NADJA SPIEGELMAN & JULIA PHILLIPS

Book Design: TRACY SUNRIZE JOHNSON

DAVID NYTRA'S artwork was drawn with a crowquill pen and india ink on board.

 Printed in Singapore by Tien Wah Press (Pte.) Ltd.

Library of Congress Cataloging-in-Publication Data:
Nytra, David, 1977–
The Secret of the Stone Frog : a TOON book / by David Nytra. p. cm.
Summary: Siblings Leah and Alan wake one morning in the middle of an enchanted forest and encounter a strange and spectacular world filled with foppish lions, giant rabbits, and a talking stone frog for a guide.
ISBN 978-1-935179-18-4
1. Graphic novels. [1. Graphic novels. 2. Fantasy. 3. Brothers and sisters--Fiction.] I. Title.
PZ7.7.N98Se 2012 741.5'973--dc23 2011050431

ISBN 13: 978-1-935179-18-4 ISBN 10: 1-935179-18-7
12 13 14 15 16 17 TWP 10 9 8 7 6 5 4 3 2 1

www.TOON-BOOKS.com

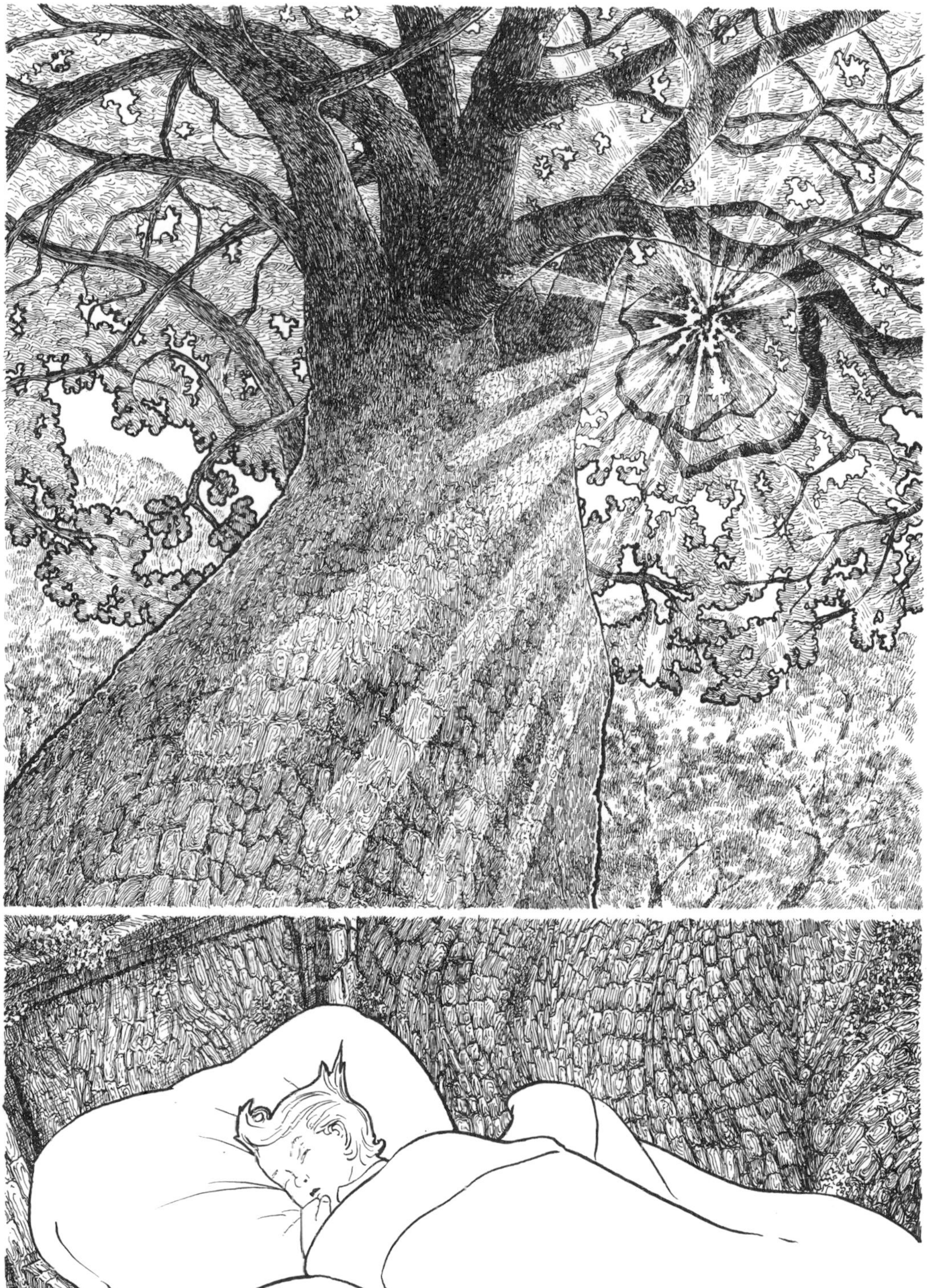

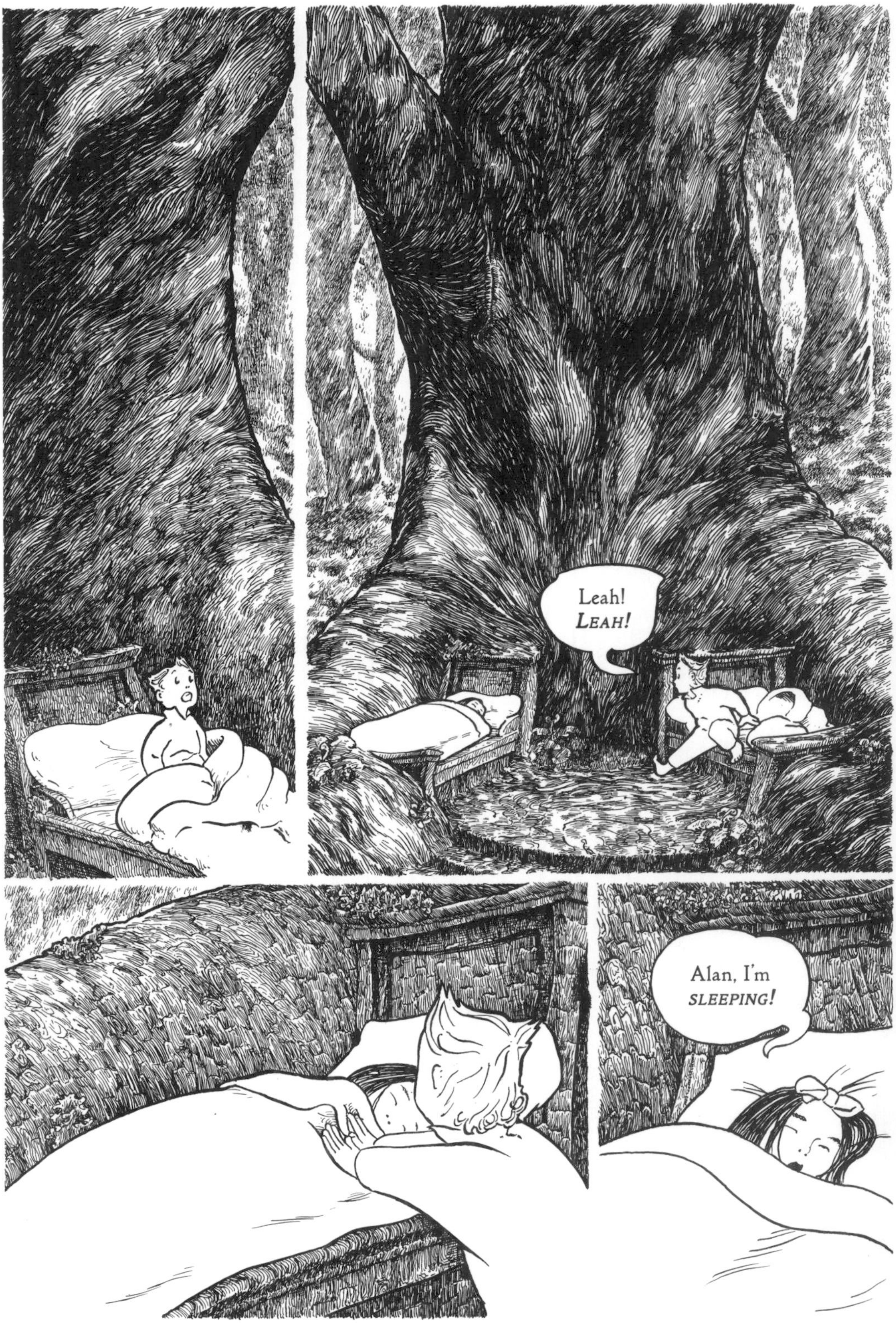
Leah!
LEAH!
Alan, I'm
SLEEPING!

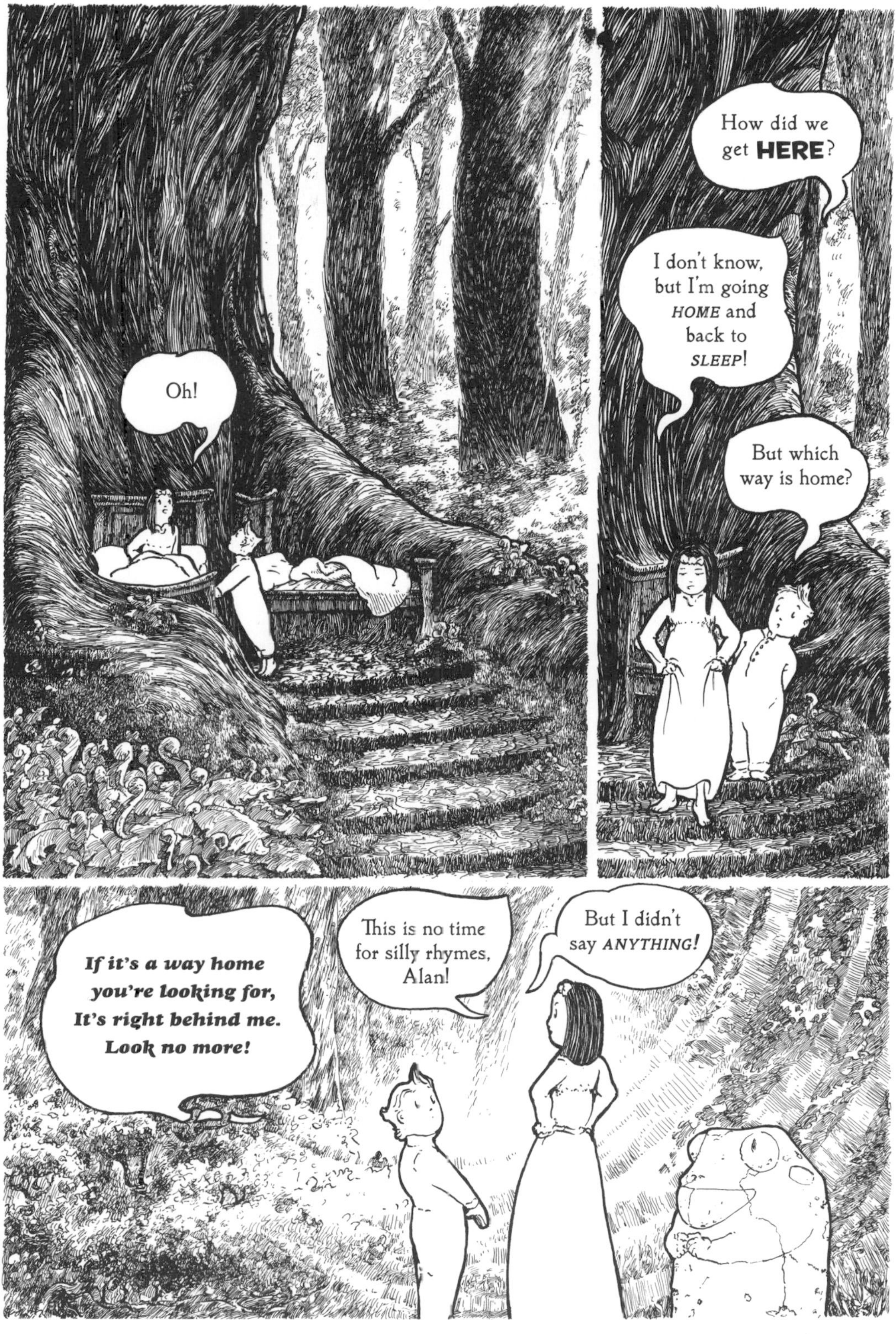
Oh!
How did we get HERE?
I don't know, but I'm going HOME and back to SLEEP!
But which way is home?
If it's a way home you're looking for, It's right behind me. Look no more!
This is no time for silly rhymes, Alan!
But I didn't say ANYTHING!

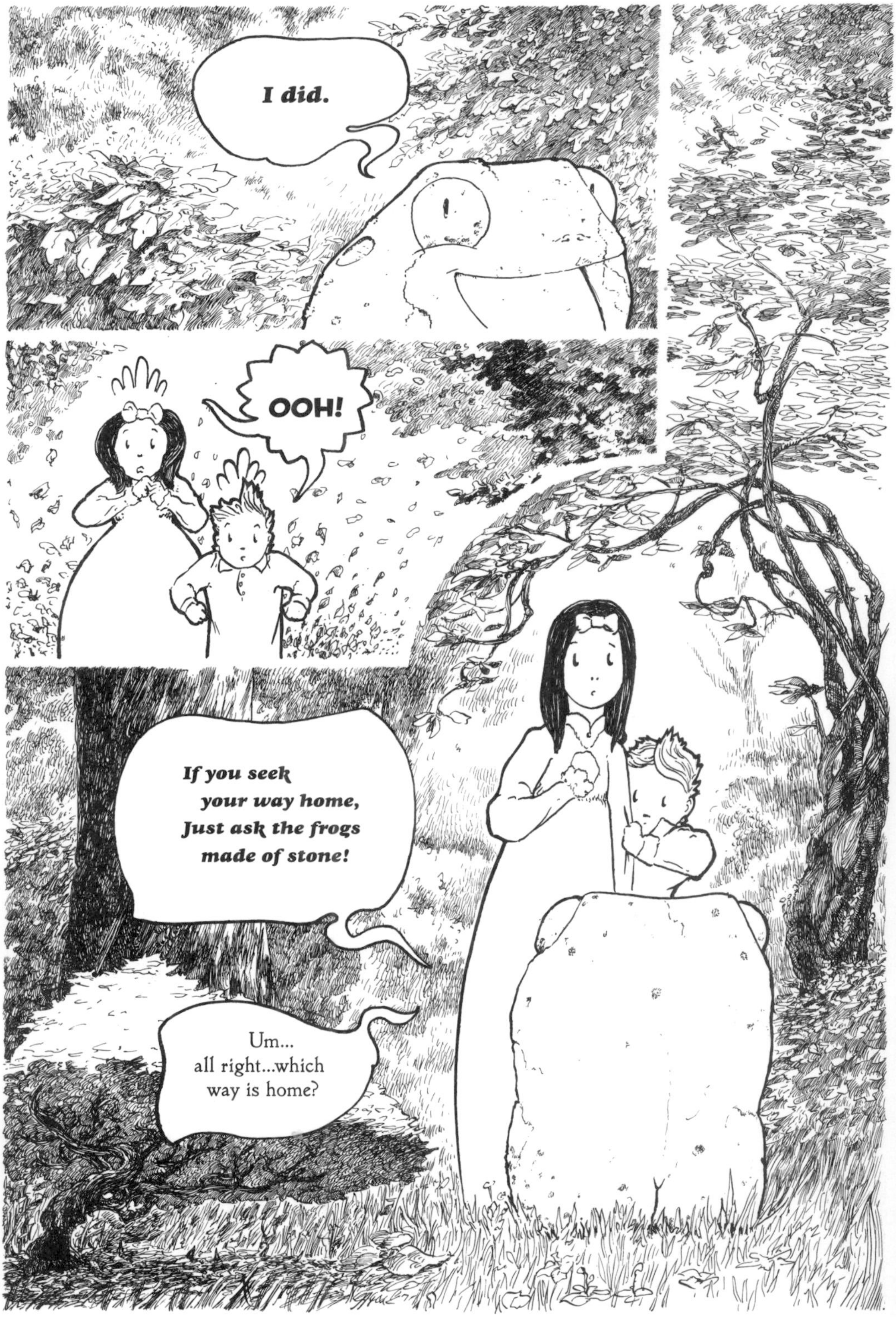
I did.
OOH!
If you seek your way home, Just ask the frogs made of stone!
Um... all right...which way is home?

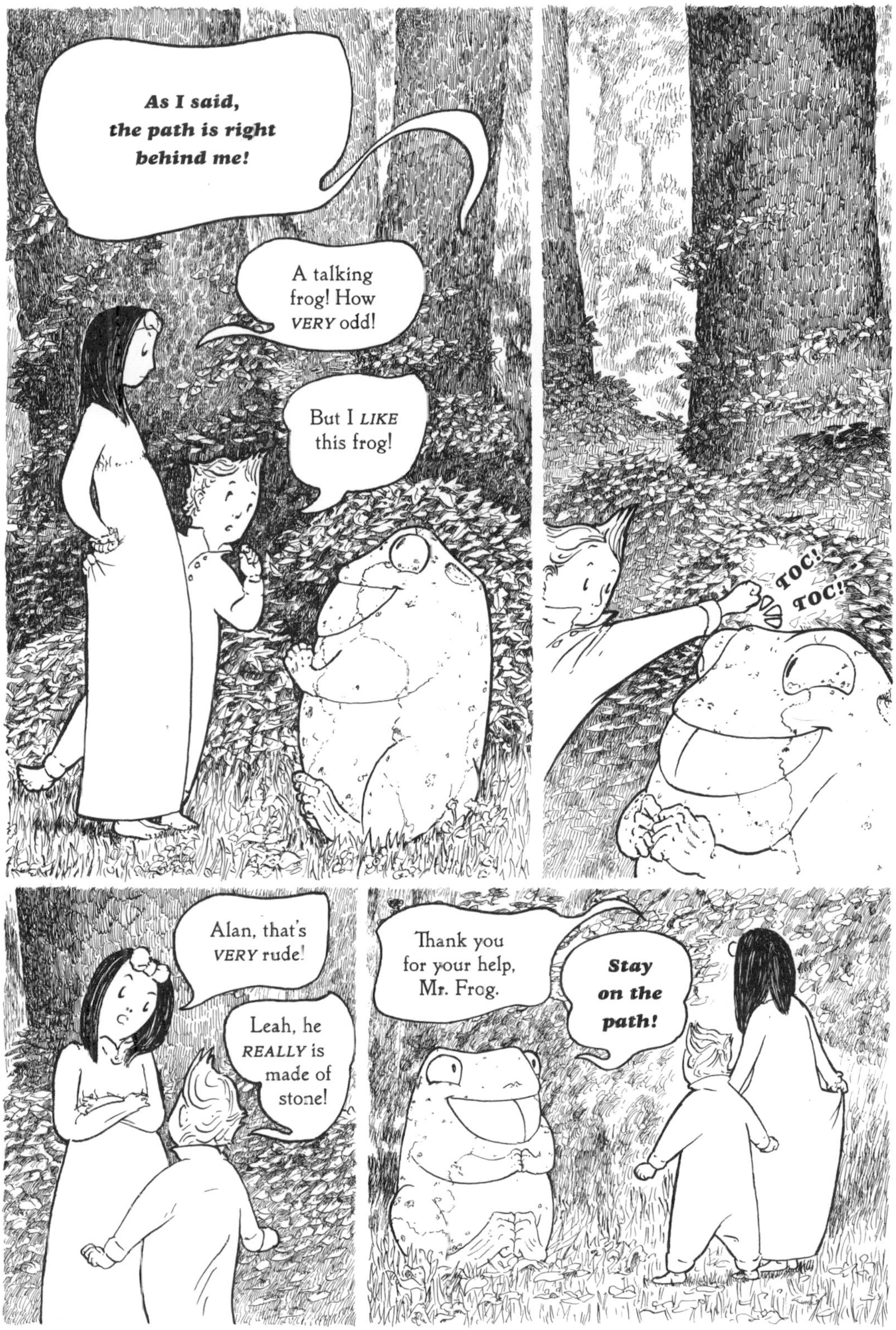

As I said, the path is right behind me!
A talking frog! How VERY odd!
But I LIKE this frog!
TOC! TOC!
Alan, that's VERY rude!
Leah, he REALLY is made of stone!
Thank you for your help, Mr. Frog.
Stay on the path!

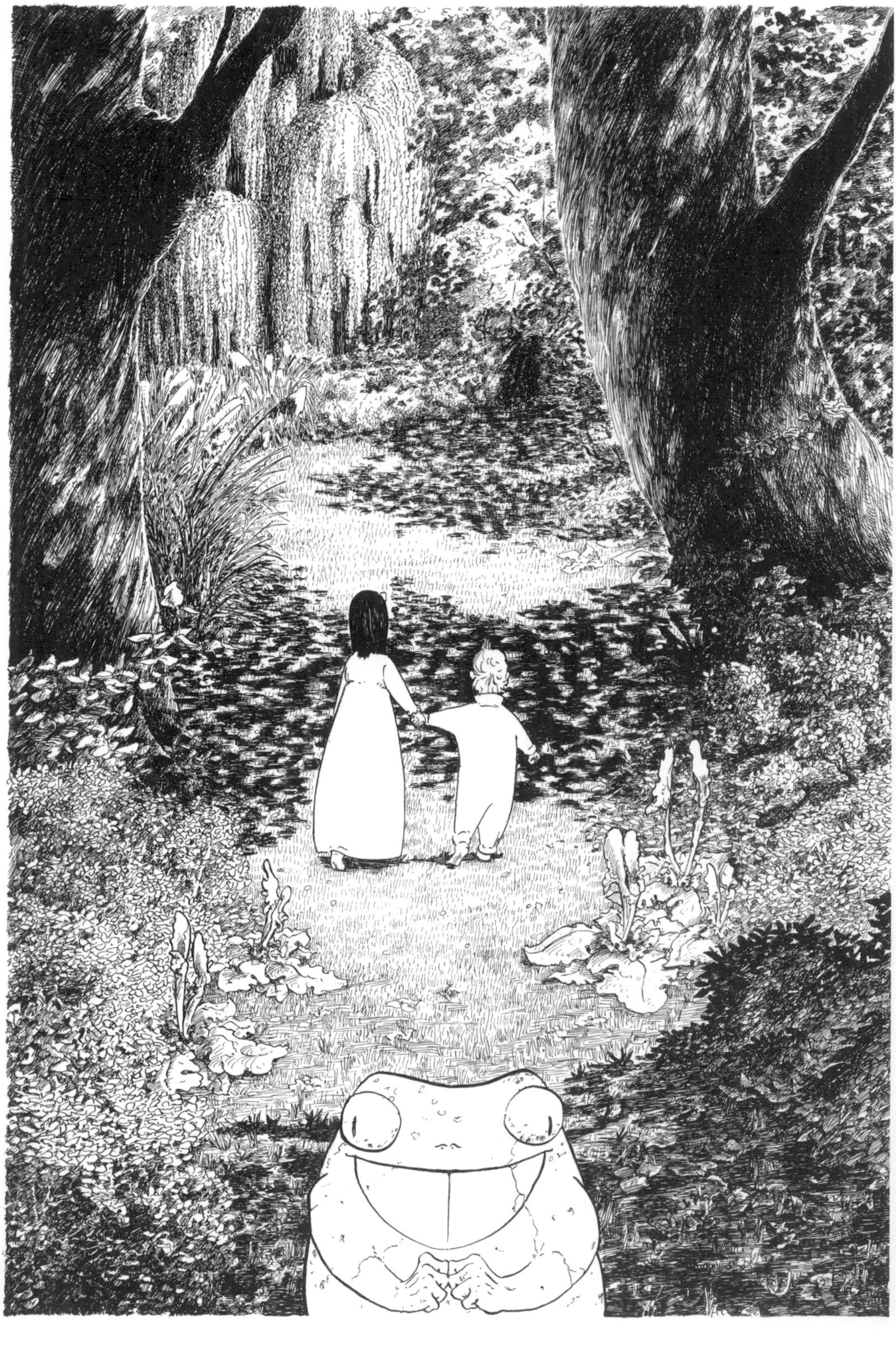

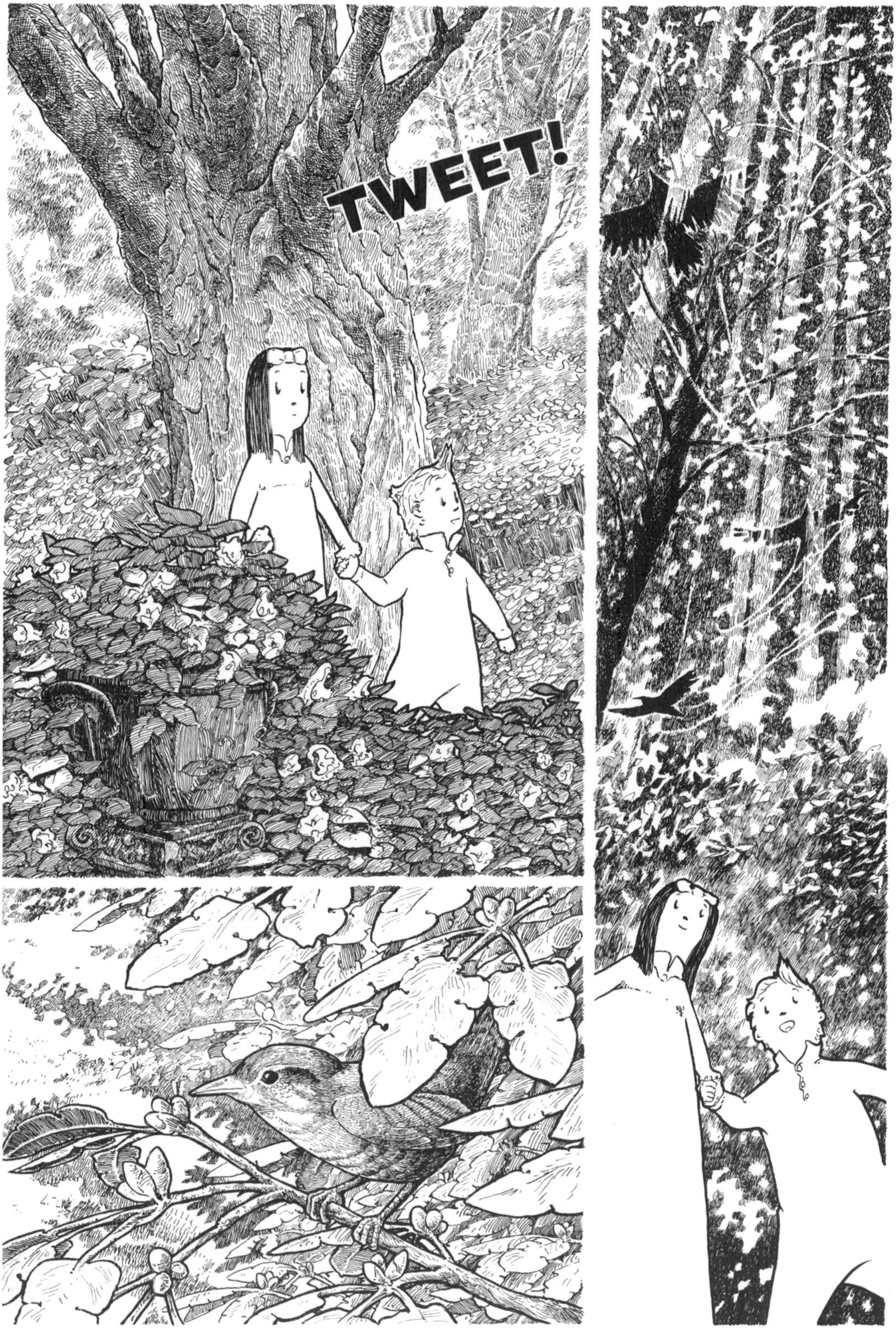
TWEET!

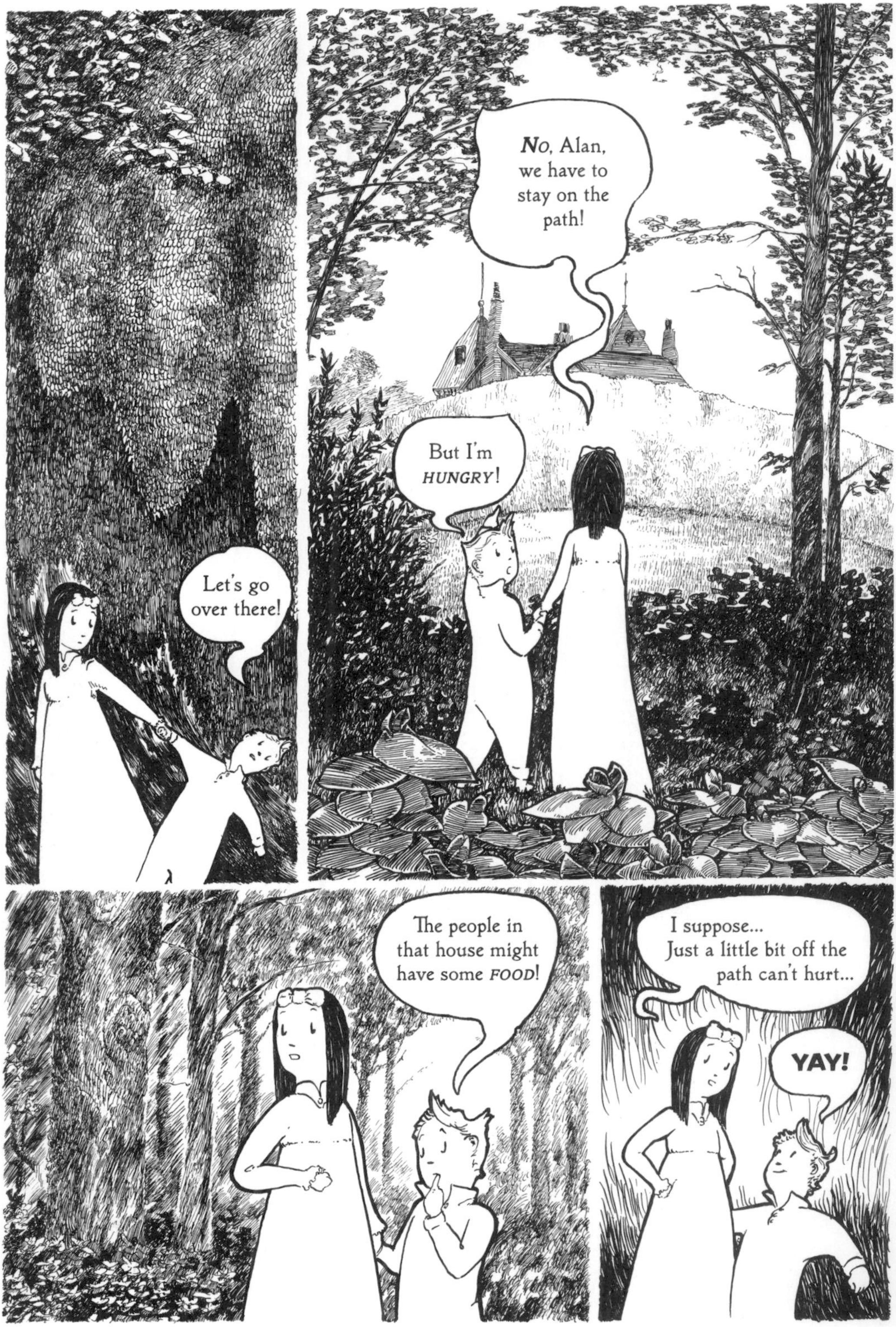
Let's go over there!
NO, Alan, we have to stay on the path!
But I'm HUNGRY!
The people in that house might have some FOOD!
I suppose... Just a little bit off the path can't hurt...
YAY!

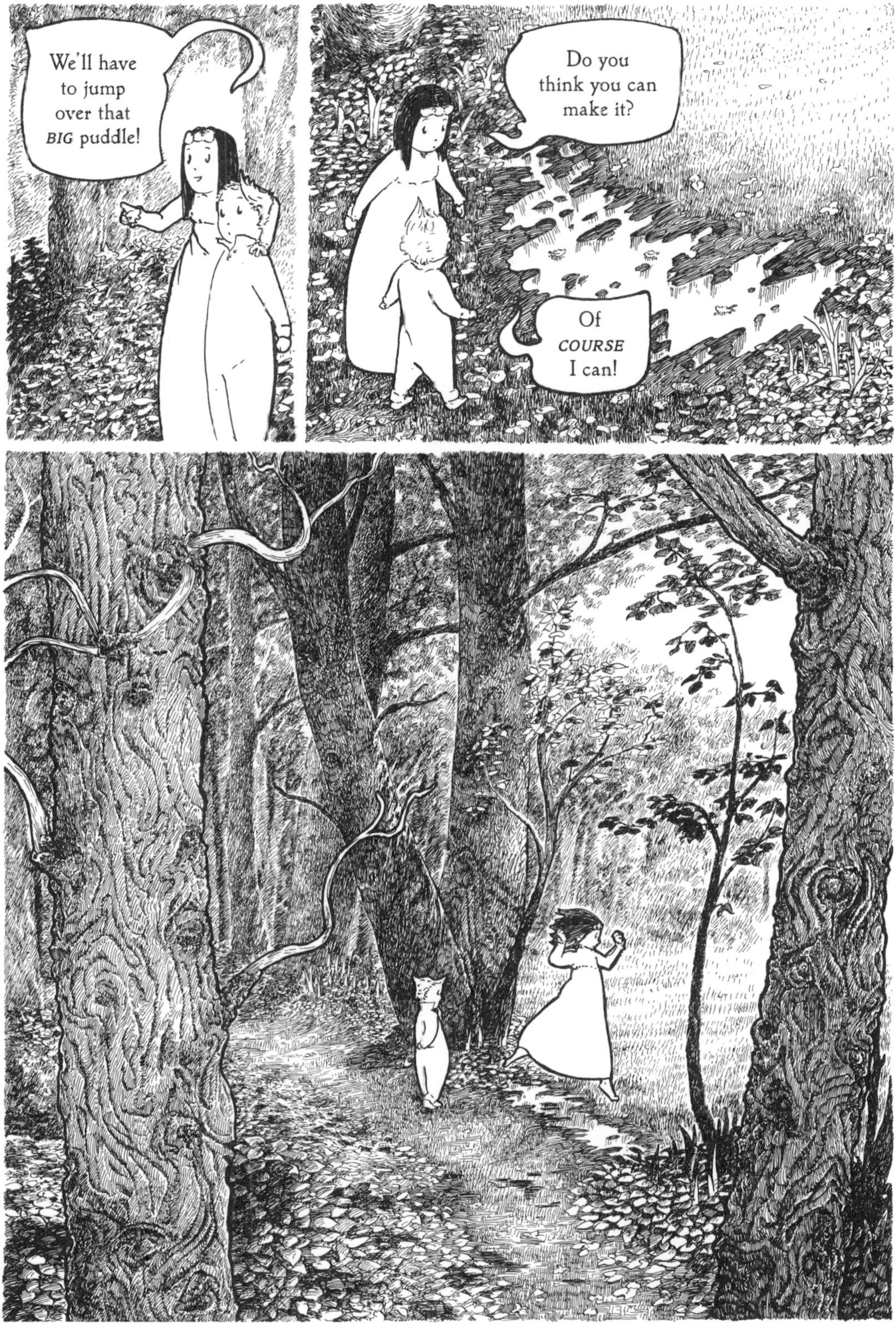
We'll have to jump over that *BIG* puddle!
Do you think you can make it?
Of *COURSE* I can!

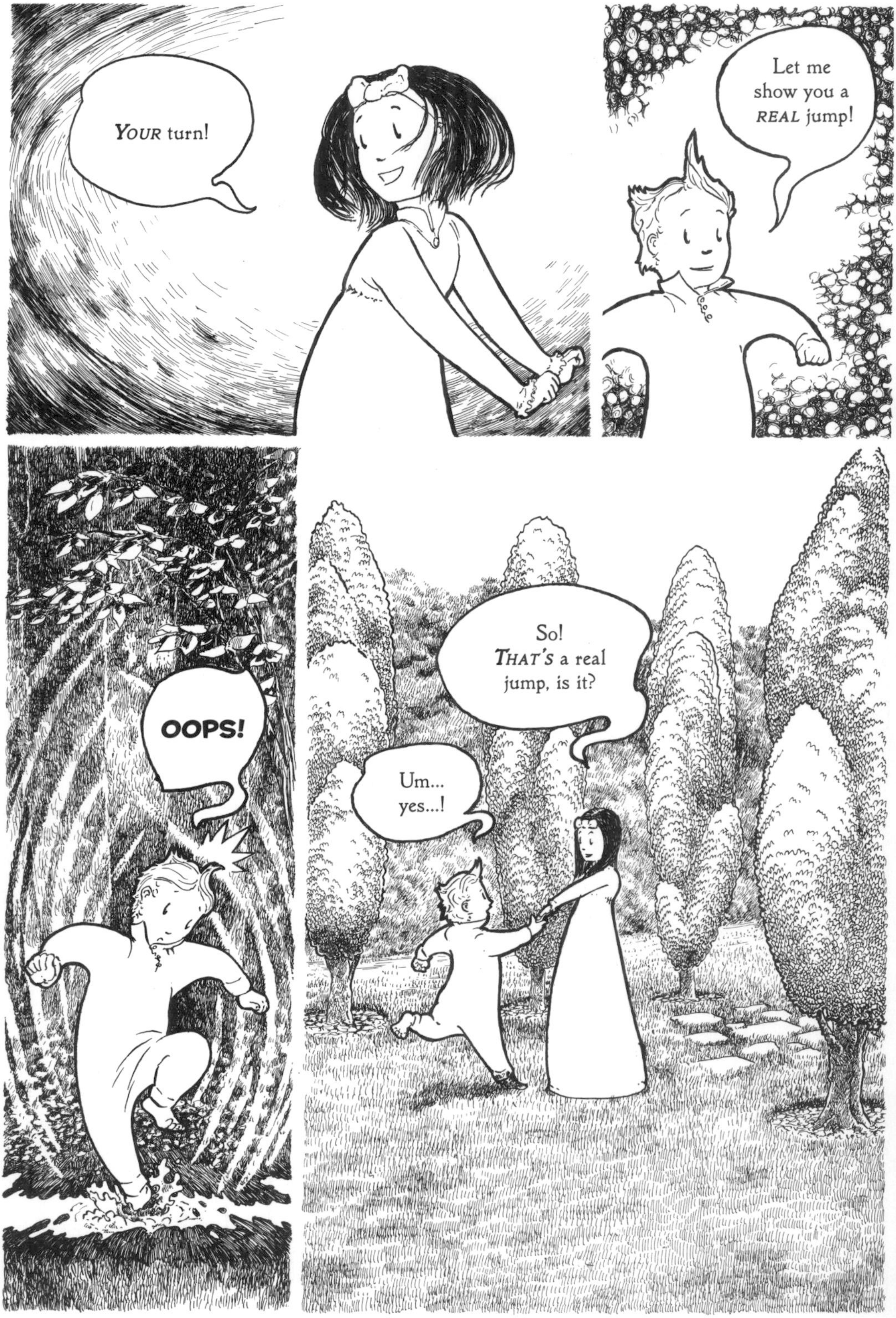
YOUR turn!
Let me show you a REAL jump!
OOPS!
So! THAT'S a real jump, is it?
Um... yes...!

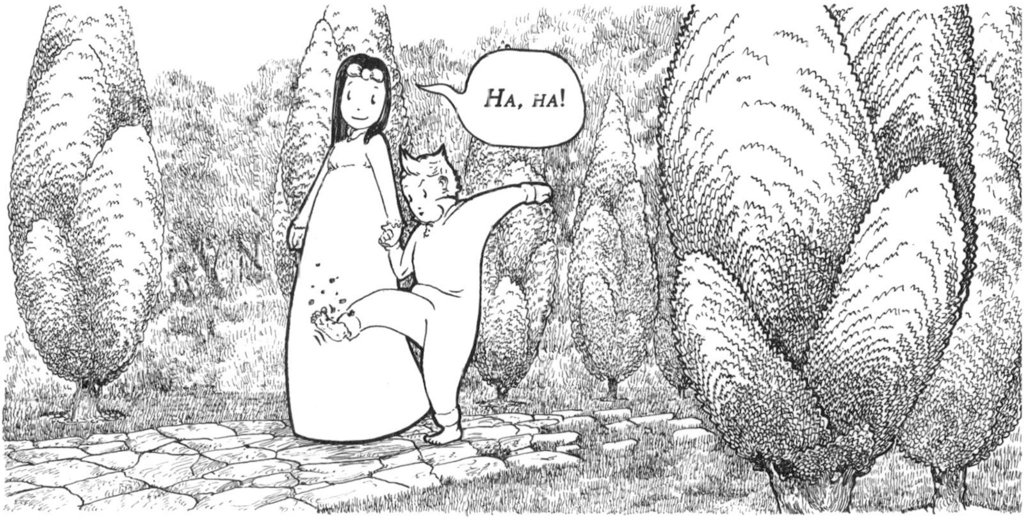
HA, HA!

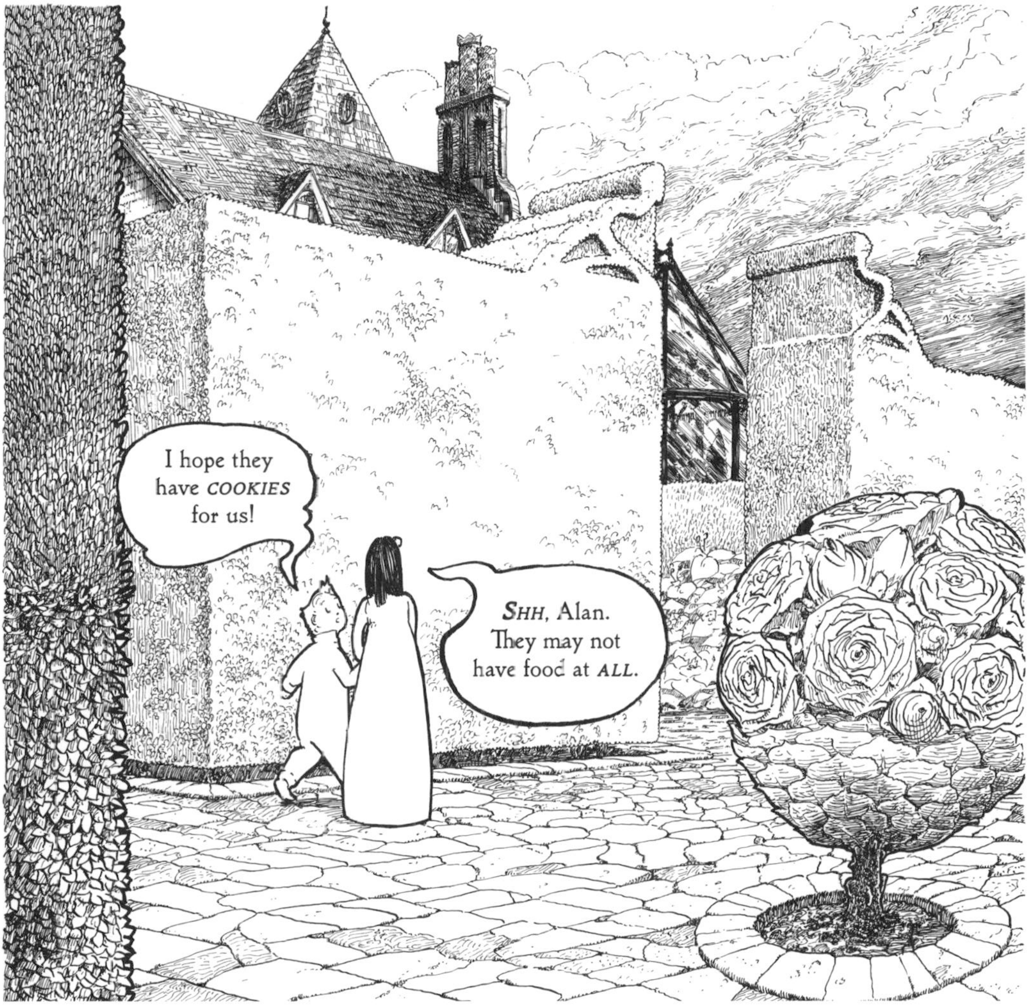
I hope they have COOKIES for us!
SHH, Alan. They may not have food at ALL.

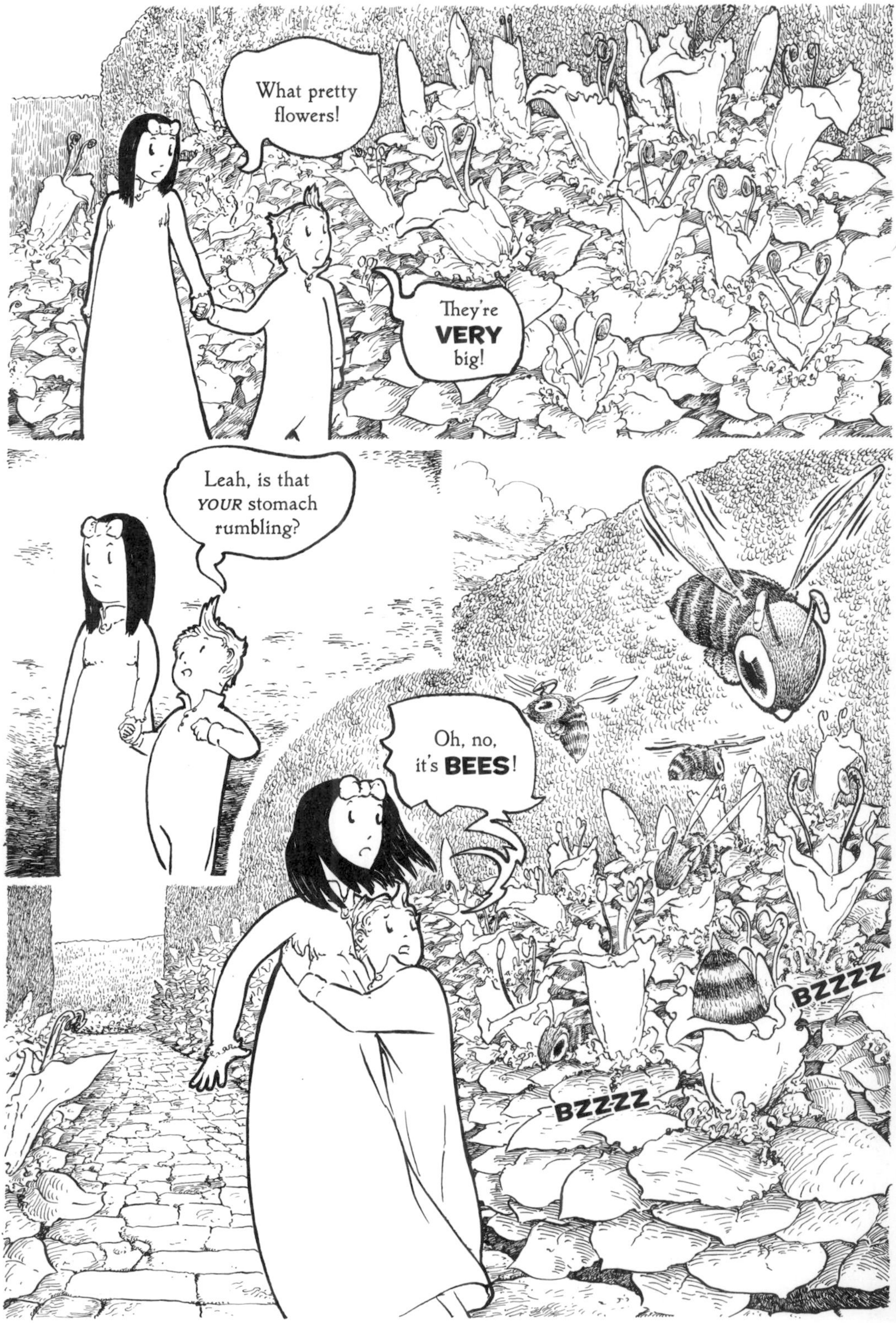
What pretty flowers!
They're **VERY** big!
Leah, is that *YOUR* stomach rumbling?
Oh, no, it's **BEES**!
BZZZZ
BZZZZ

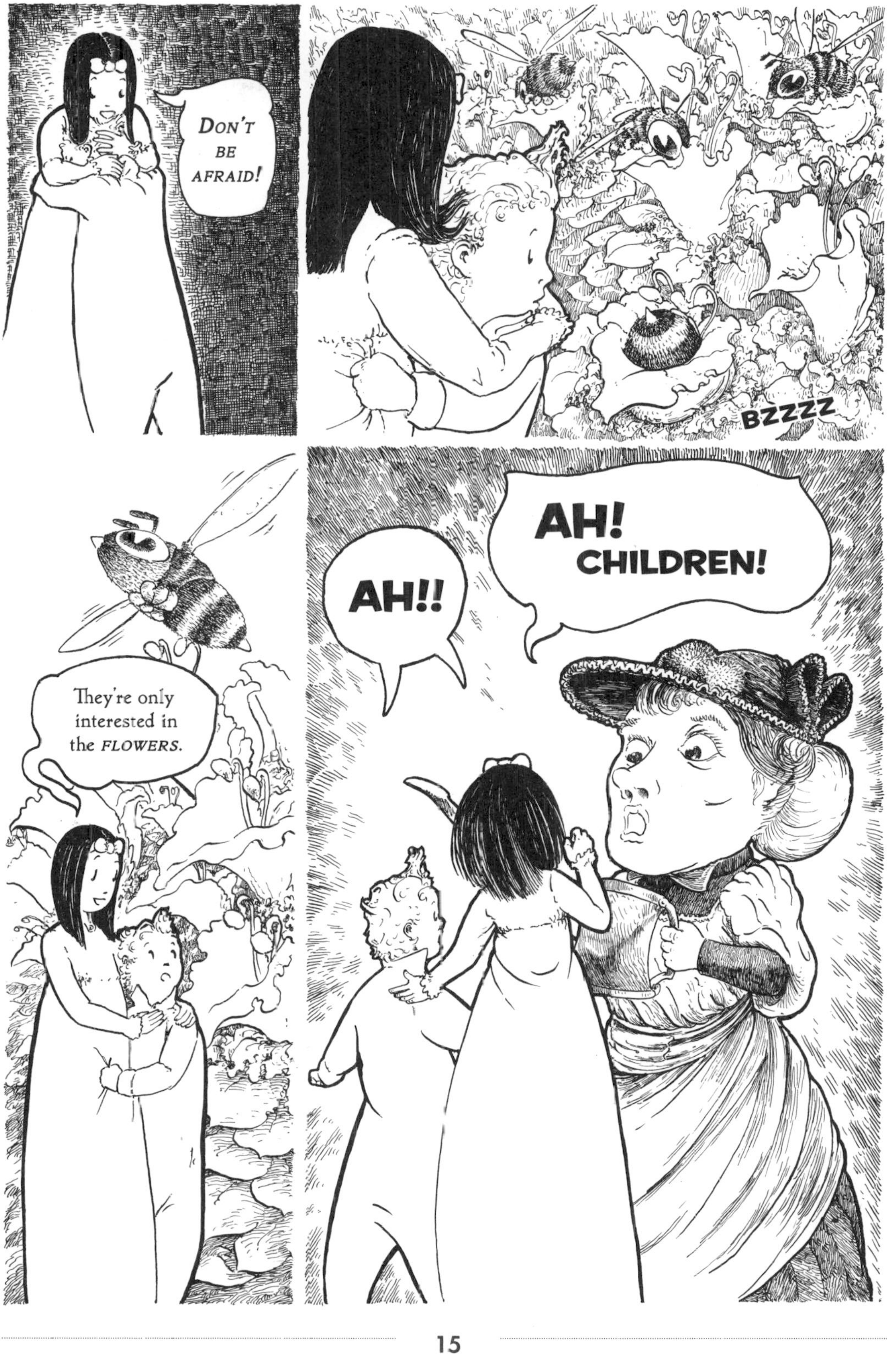
DON'T BE AFRAID!
BZZZZ
They're only interested in the FLOWERS.
AH!!
AH! CHILDREN!

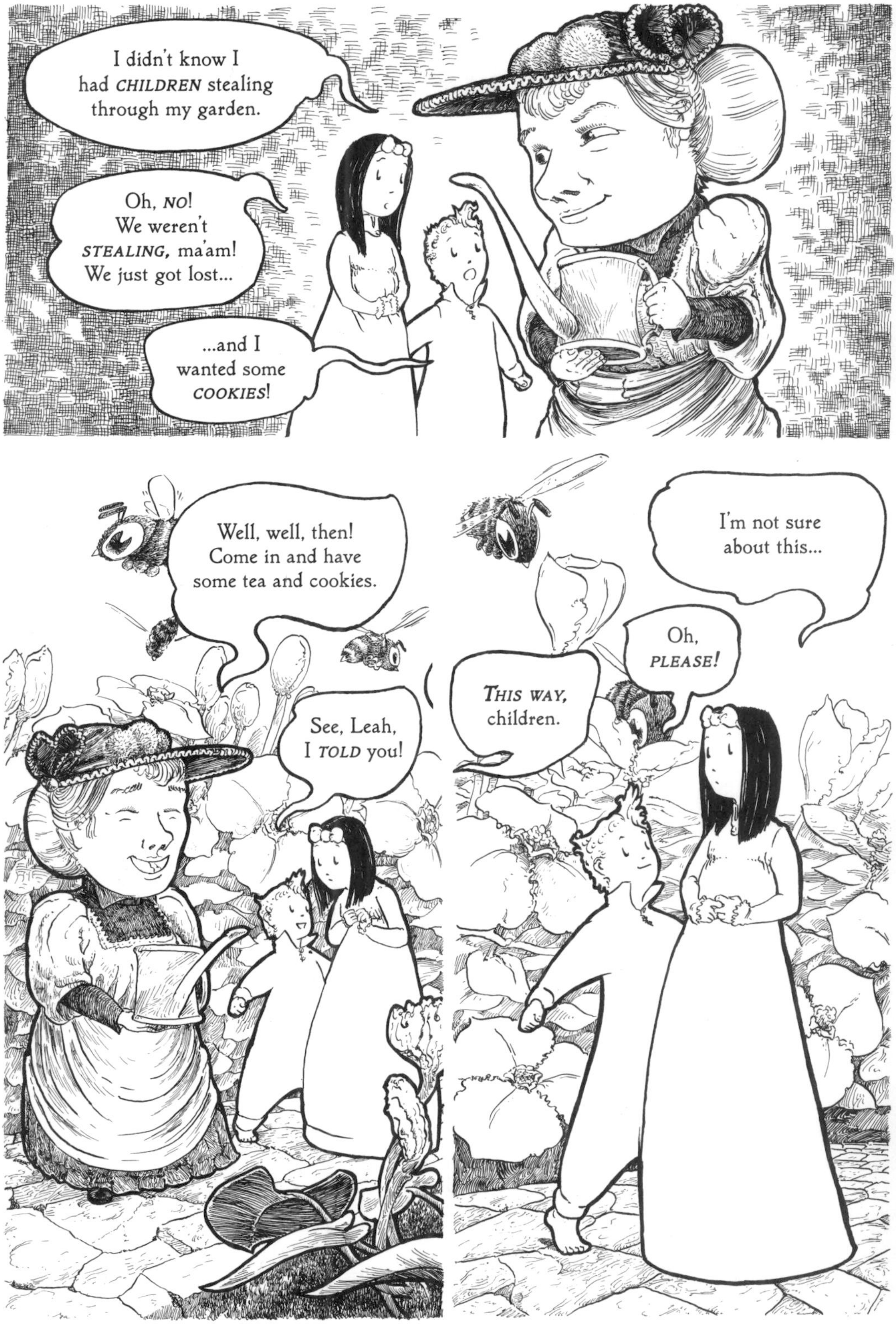

I didn't know I had CHILDREN stealing through my garden.
Oh, NO! We weren't STEALING, ma'am! We just got lost...
...and I wanted some COOKIES!
Well, well, then! Come in and have some tea and cookies.
See, Leah, I TOLD you!
THIS WAY, children.
I'm not sure about this...
Oh, PLEASE!

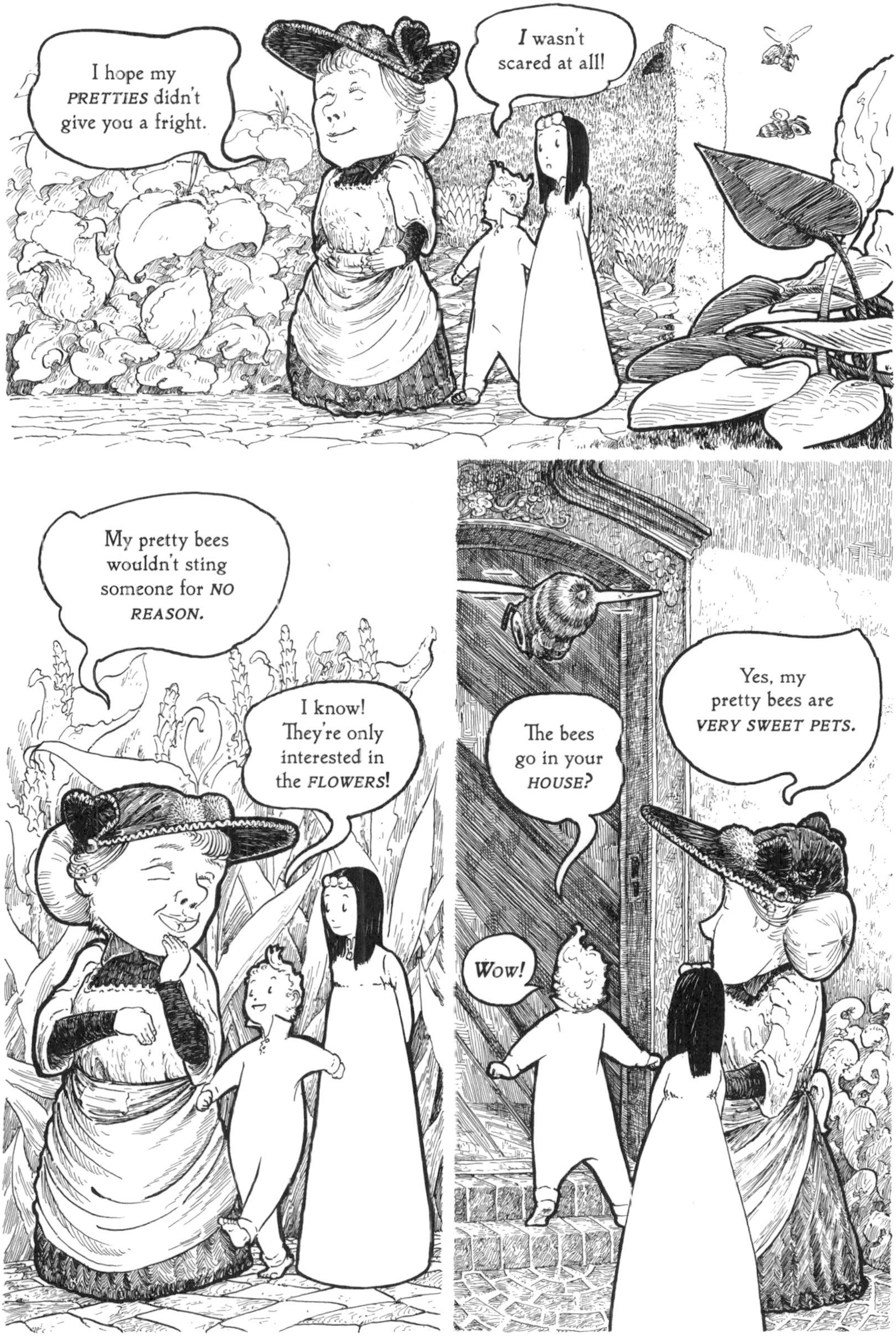
I hope my PRETTIES didn't give you a fright.
I wasn't scared at all!
My pretty bees wouldn't sting someone for NO REASON.
I know! They're only interested in the FLOWERS!
The bees go in your HOUSE?
Yes, my pretty bees are VERY SWEET PETS.
Wow!

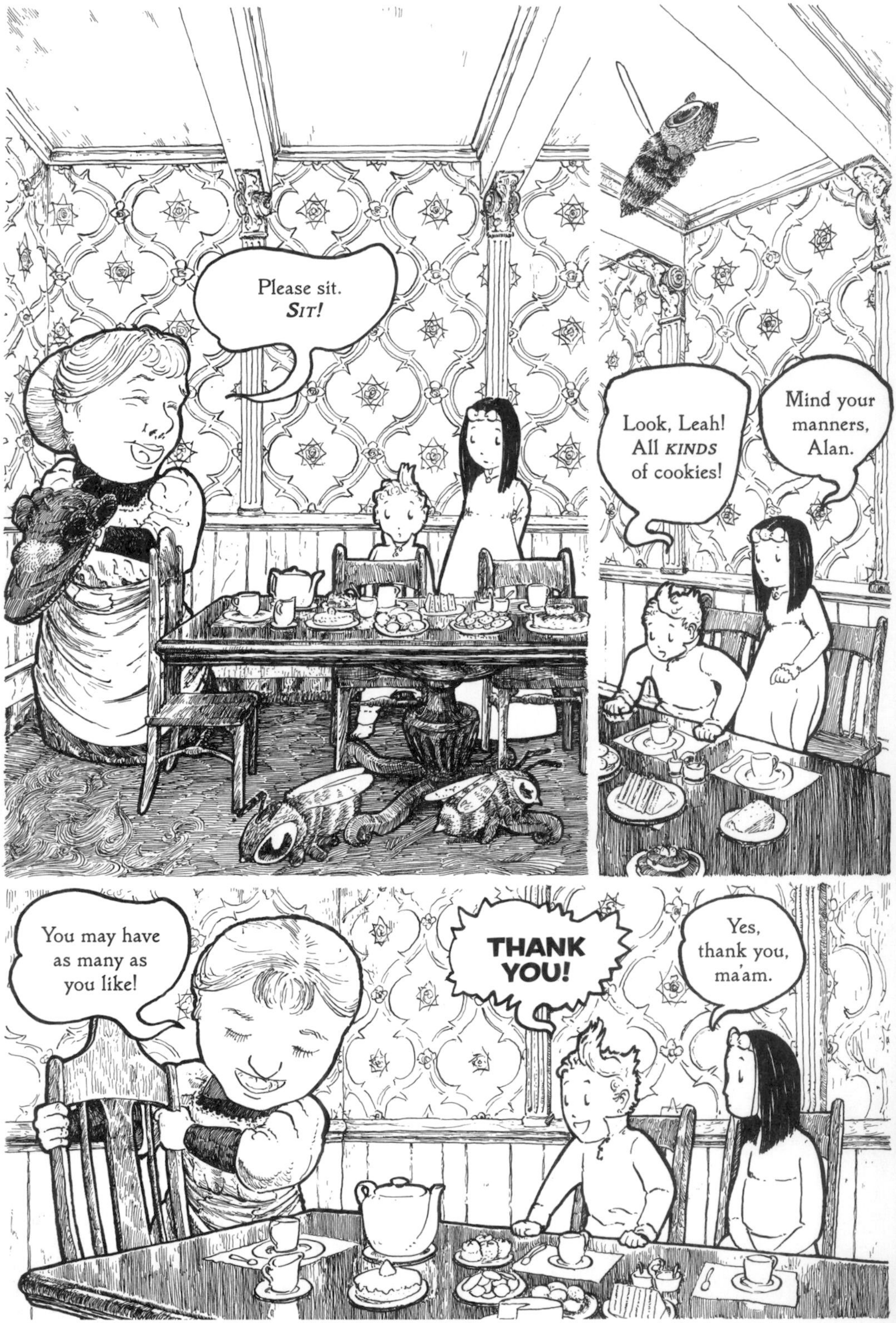
Please sit.
SIT!
Look, Leah! All *KINDS* of cookies!
Mind your manners, Alan.
You may have as many as you like!
THANK YOU!
Yes, thank you, ma'am.

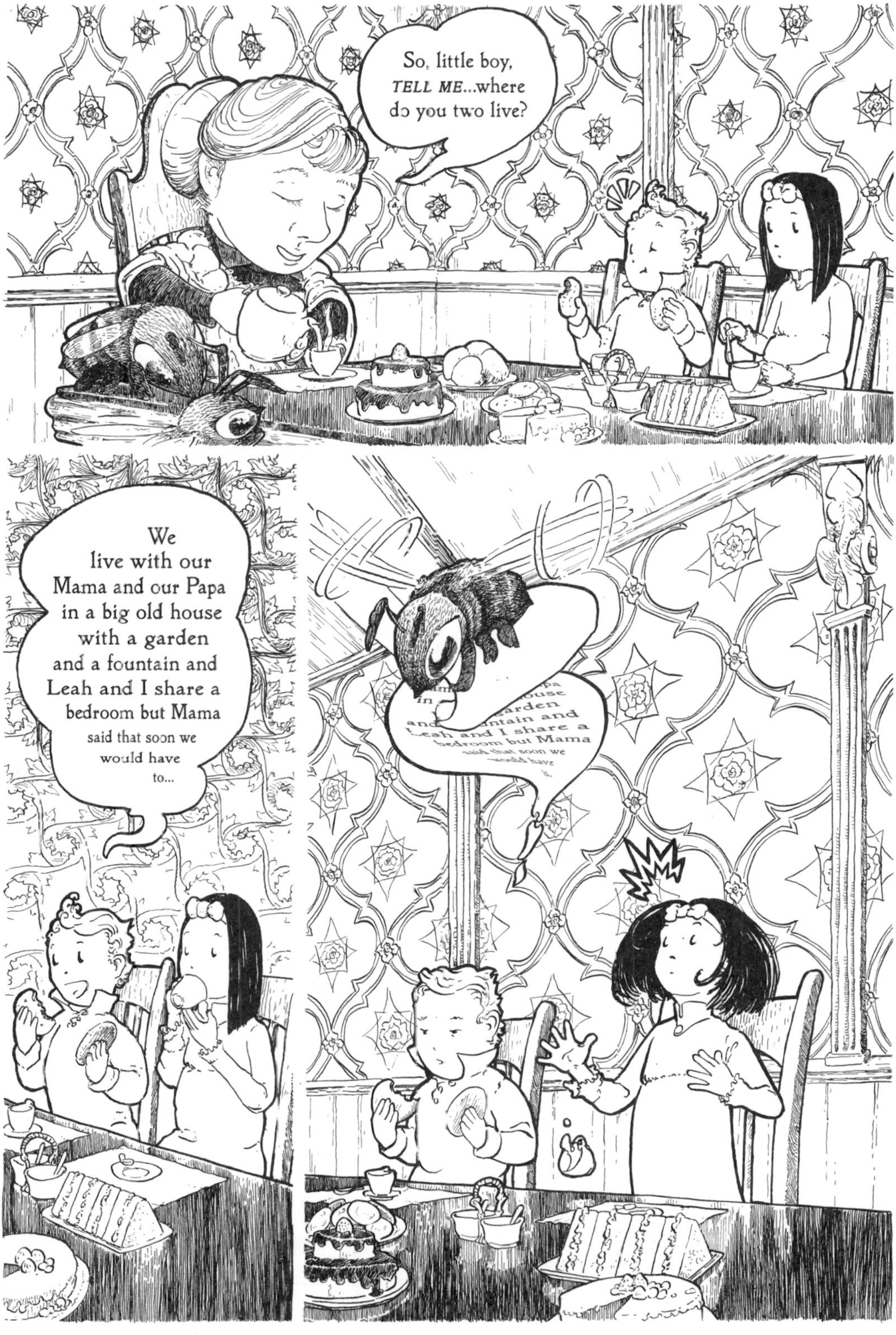
So, little boy, *TELL ME*...where do you two live?
We live with our Mama and our Papa in a big old house with a garden and a fountain and Leah and I share a bedroom but Mama said that soon we would have to...

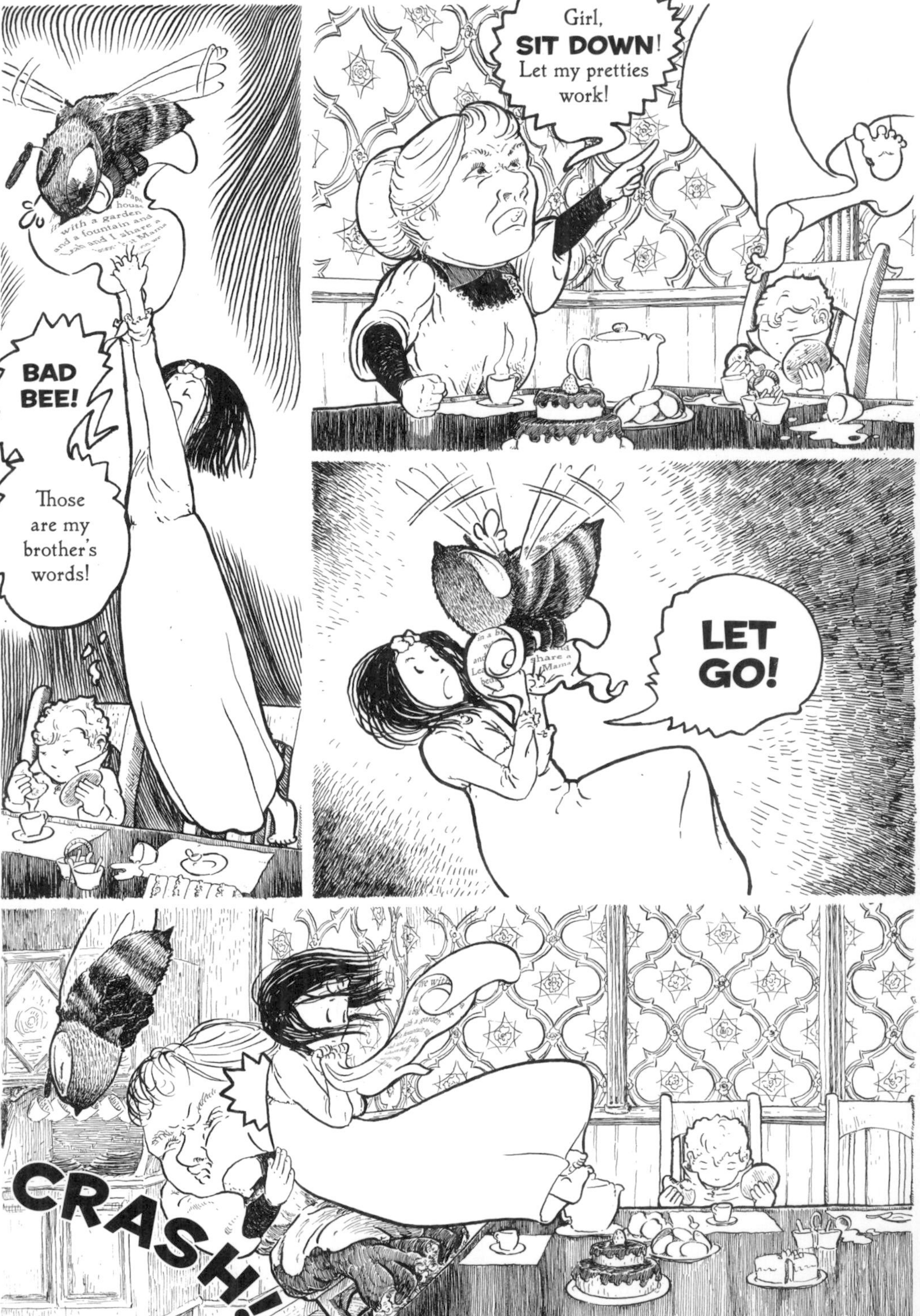
BAD BEE!
Those are my brother's words!
Girl, SIT DOWN! Let my pretties work!
LET GO!
CRASH!

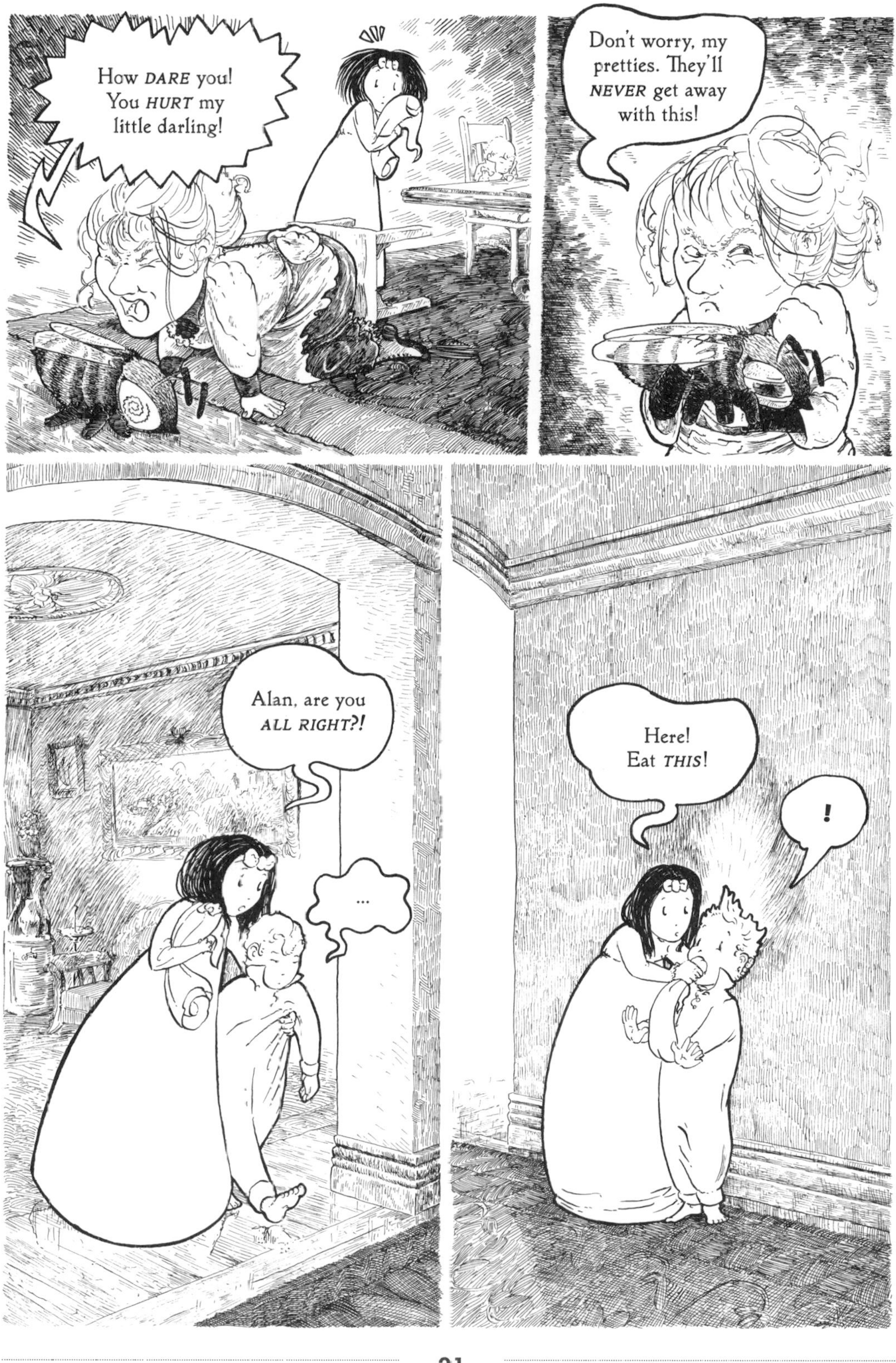
How DARE you! You HURT my little darling!
Don't worry, my pretties. They'll NEVER get away with this!
Alan, are you ALL RIGHT?!
...
Here! Eat THIS!
!

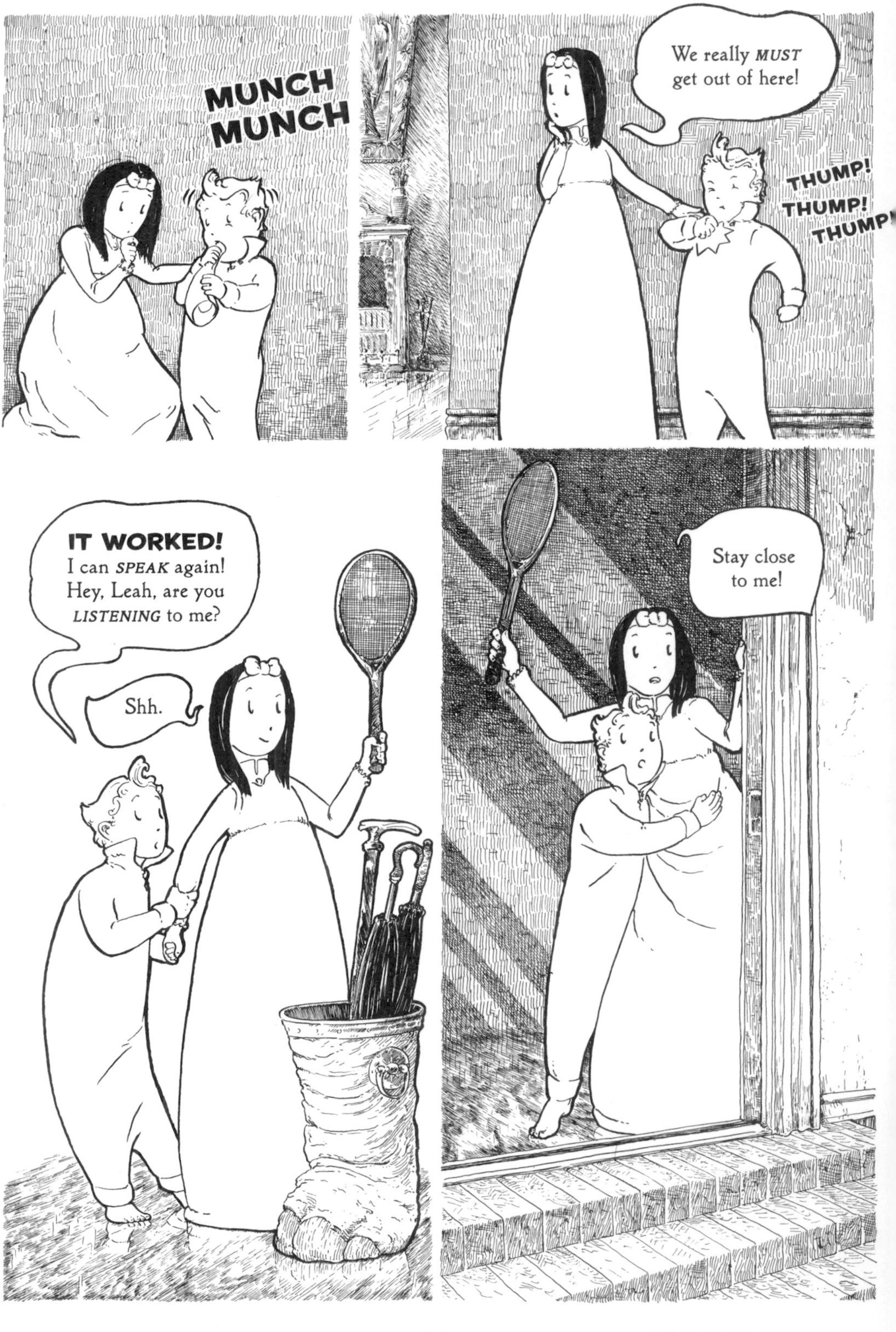

MUNCH
MUNCH
We really MUST get out of here!
THUMP!
THUMP!
THUMP!
IT WORKED! I can SPEAK again! Hey, Leah, are you LISTENING to me?
Shh.
Stay close to me!

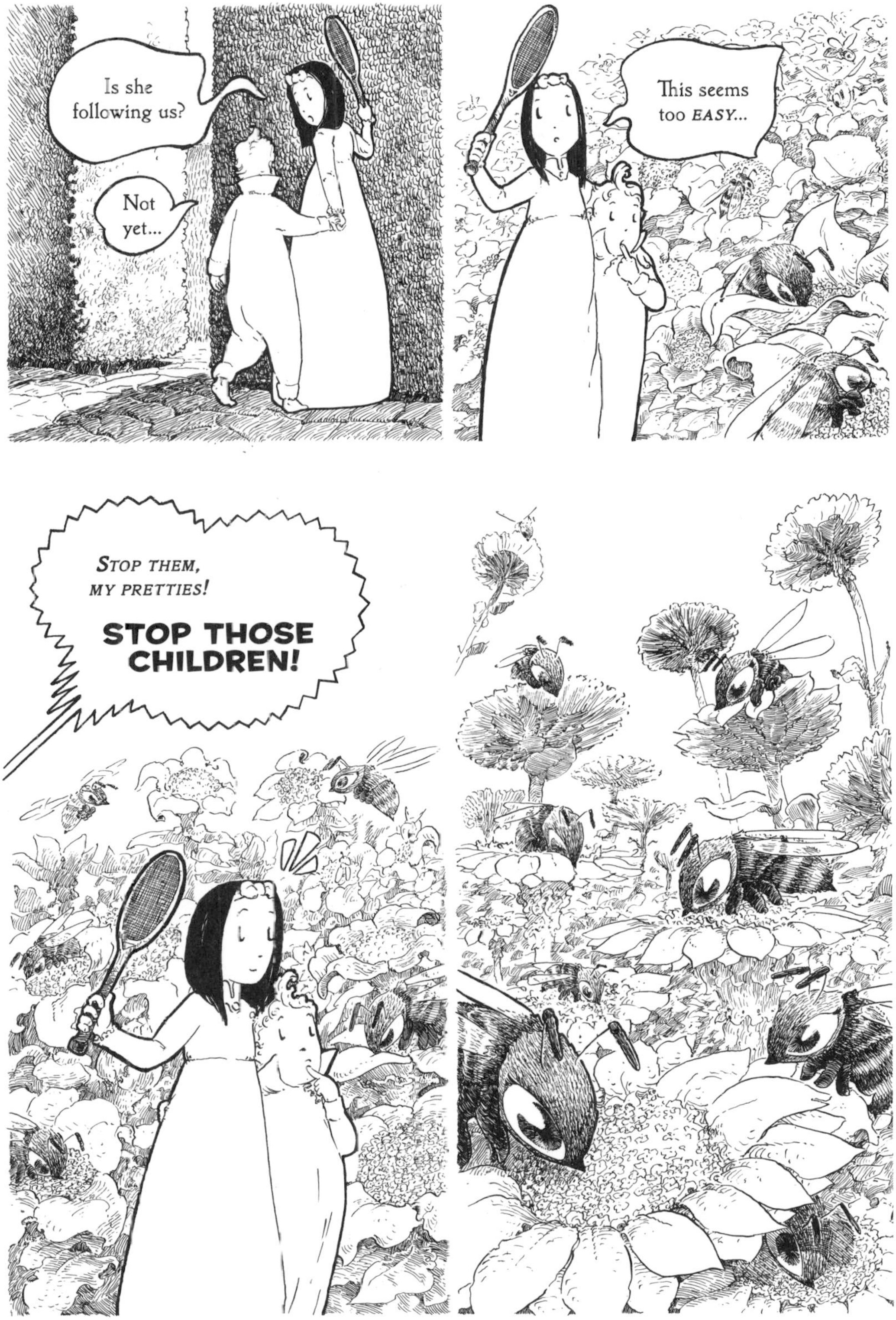
Is she following us?
Not yet...
This seems too *EASY*...
STOP THEM, MY PRETTIES!
STOP THOSE CHILDREN!

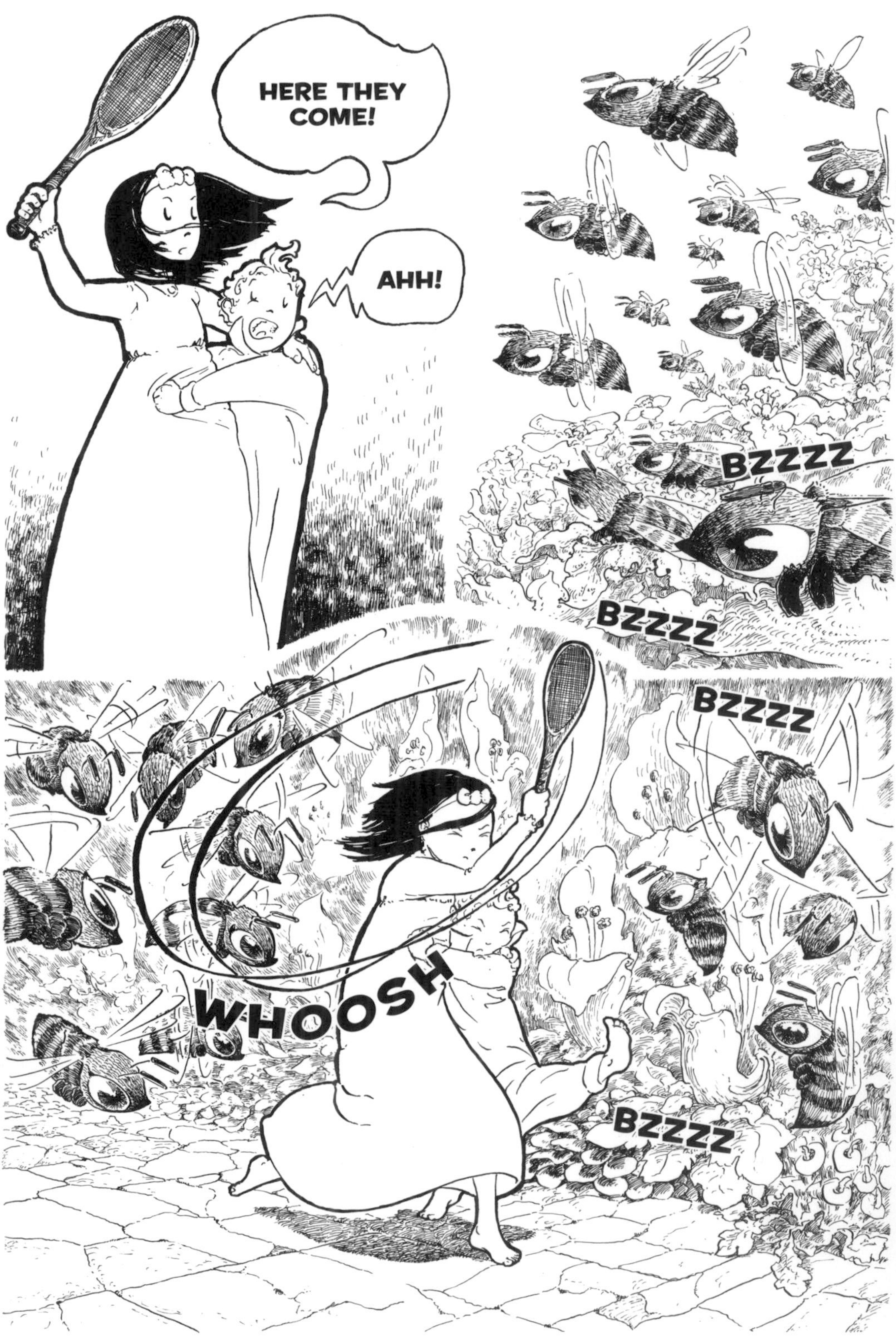
HERE THEY COME!
AHH!
BZZZZ
BZZZZ
BZZZZ
WHOOSH
BZZZZ

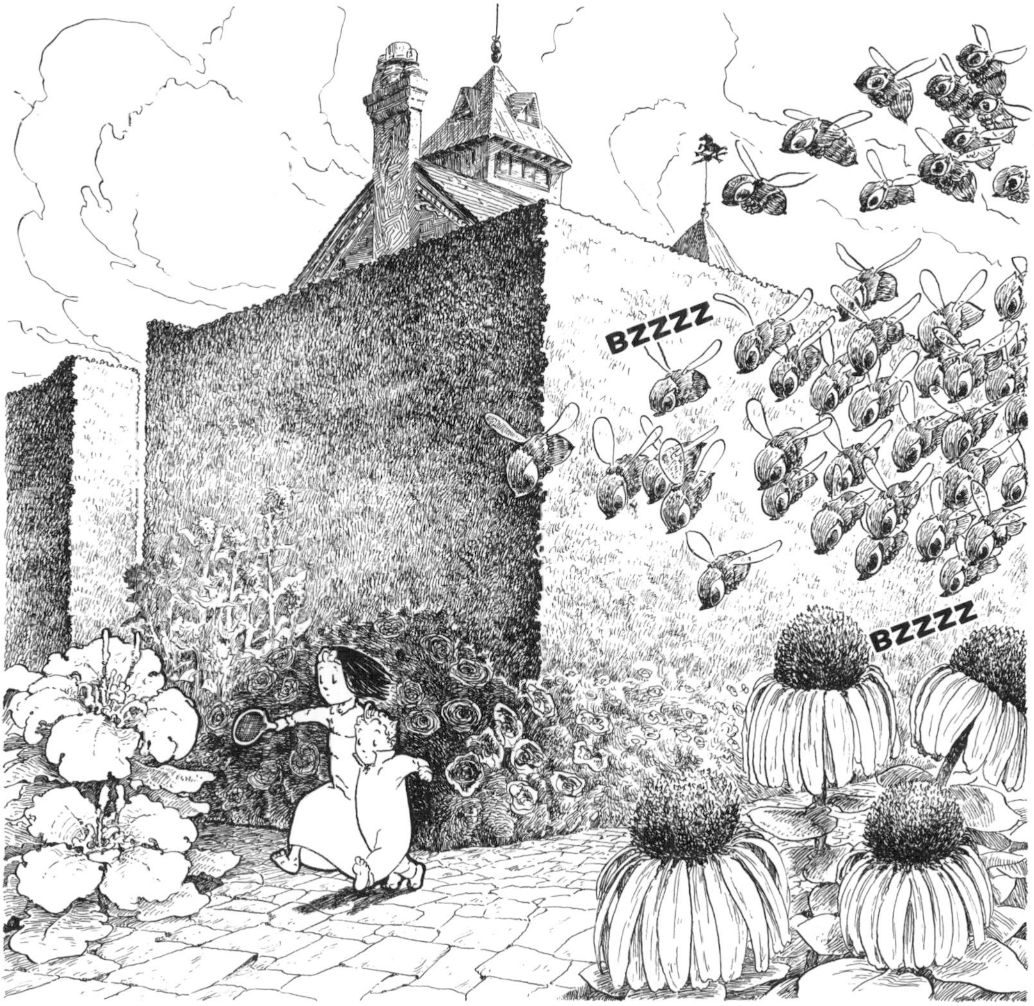
BZZZZ
BZZZZ

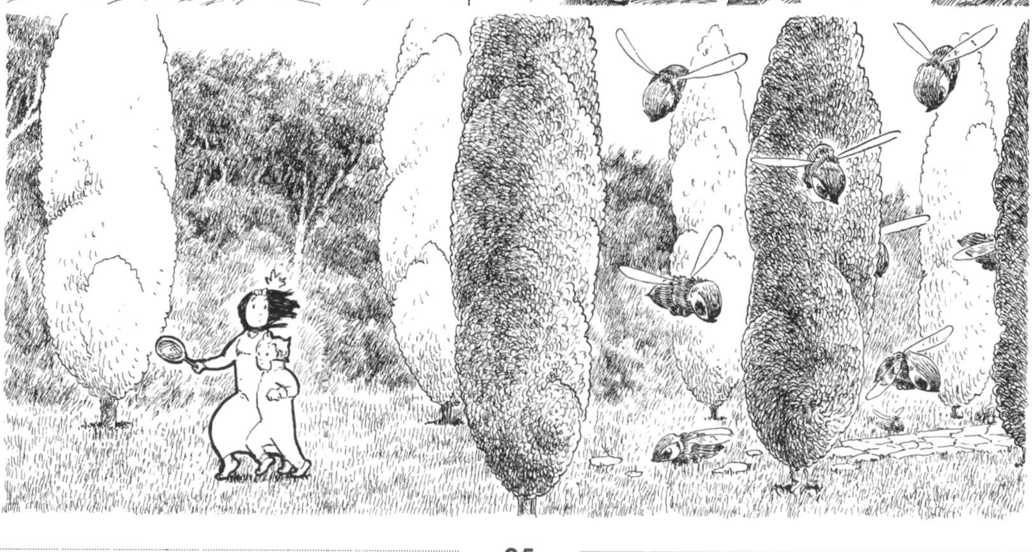

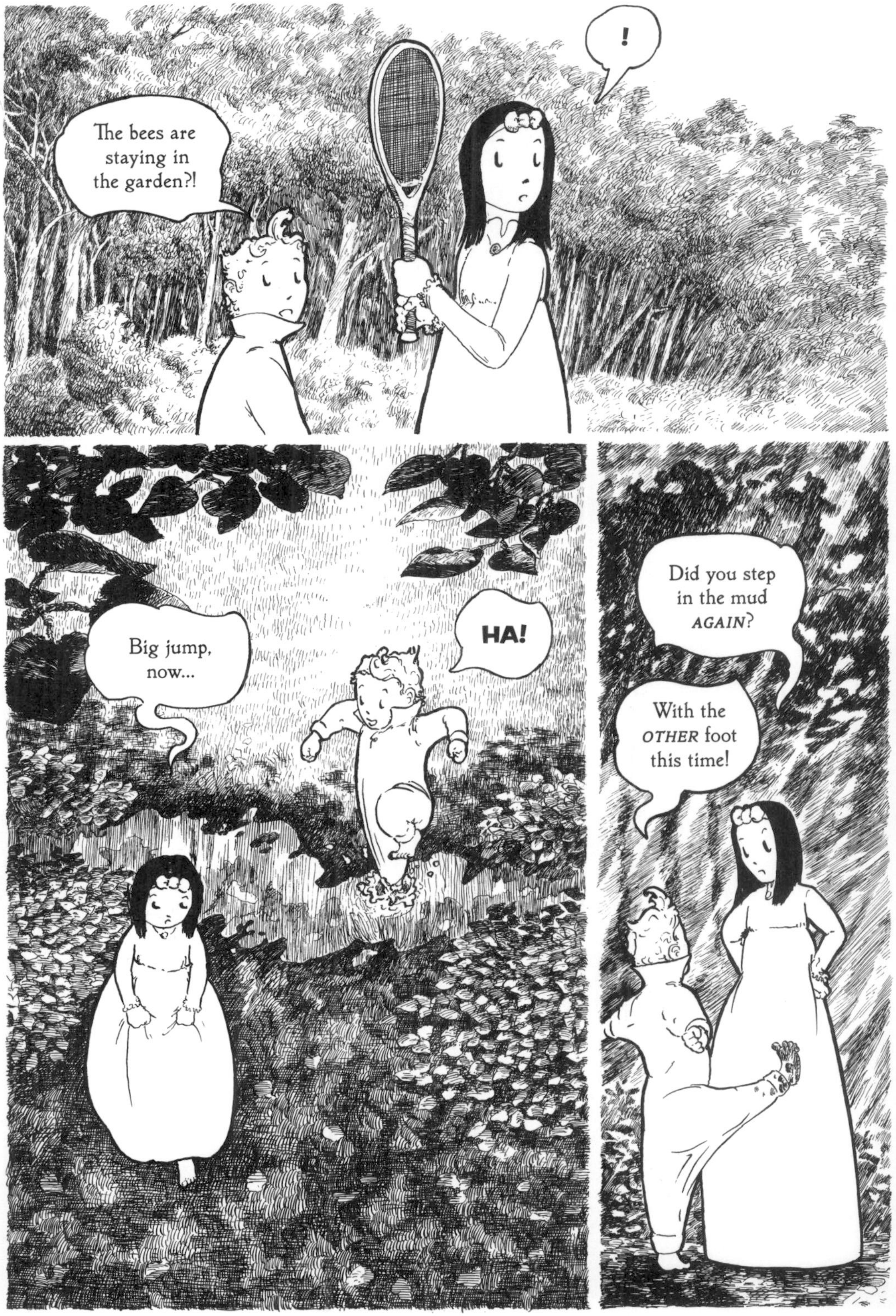
The bees are staying in the garden?!
!
Big jump, now...
HA!
Did you step in the mud AGAIN?
With the OTHER foot this time!

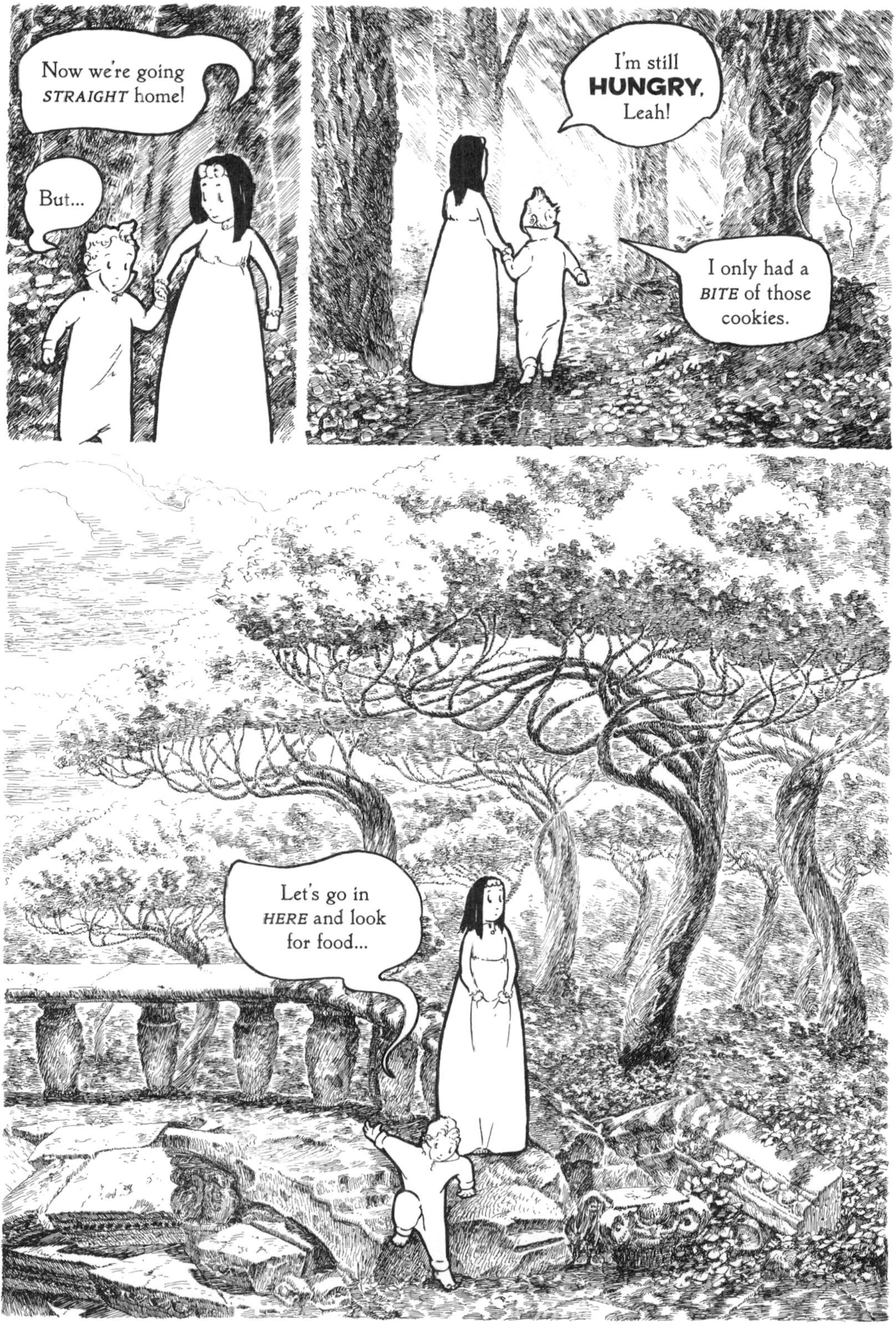
Now we're going STRAIGHT home!
But...
I'm still HUNGRY, Leah!
I only had a BITE of those cookies.
Let's go in HERE and look for food...

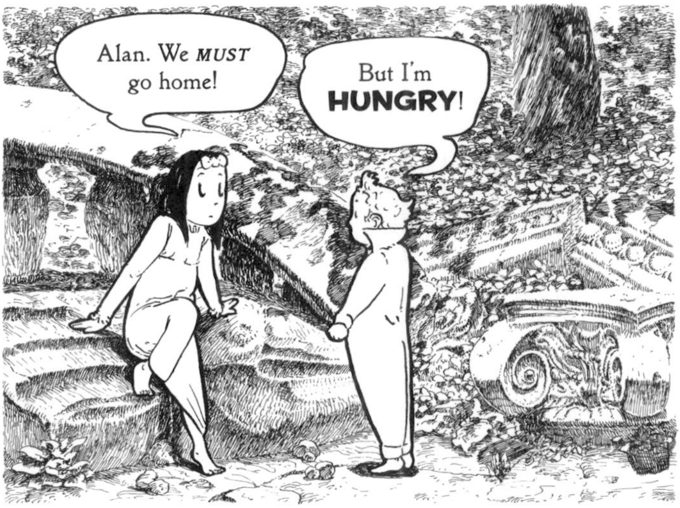
Alan. We *MUST* go home!
But I'm **HUNGRY**!

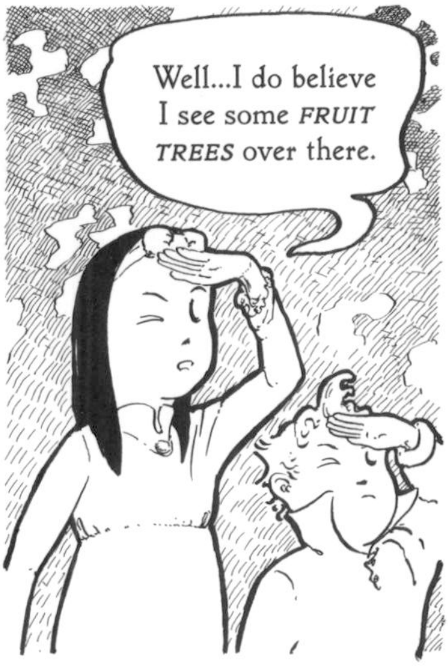
Well...I do believe I see some *FRUIT TREES* over there.

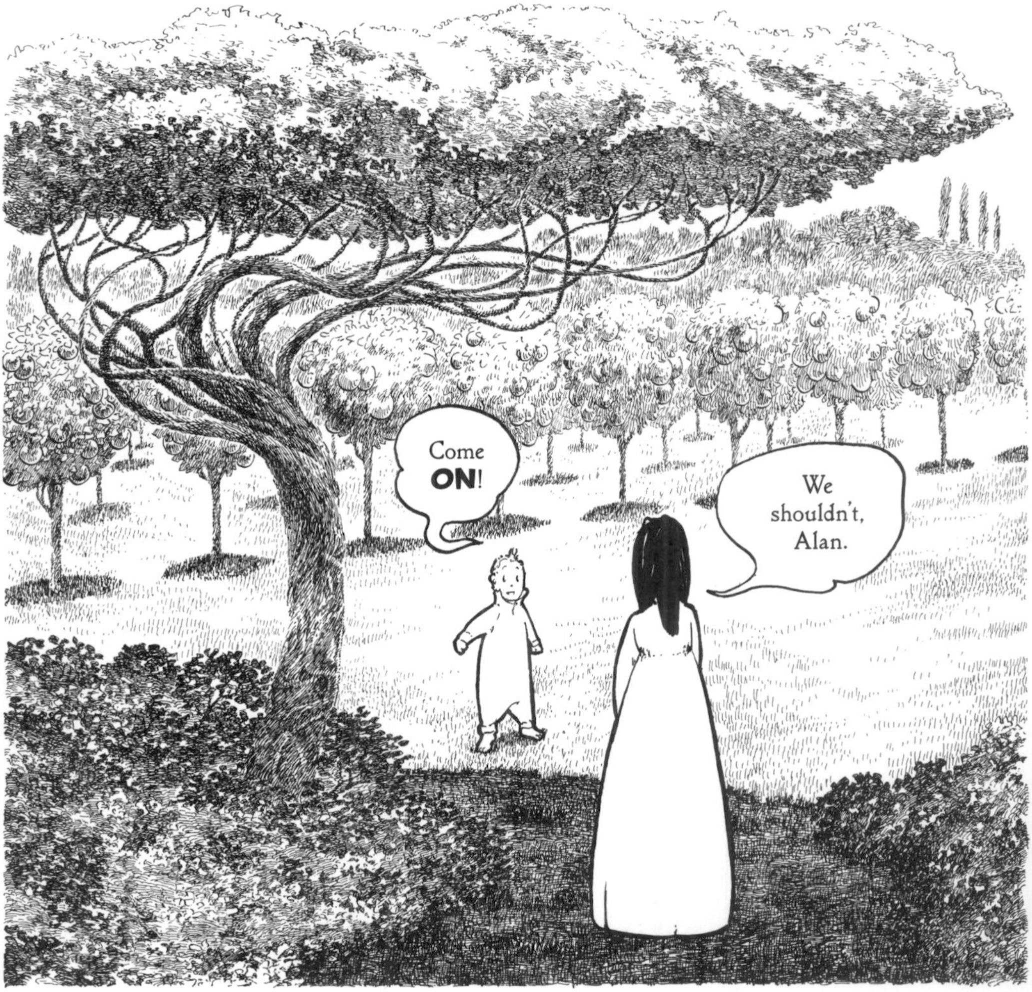
Come **ON**!
We shouldn't, Alan.

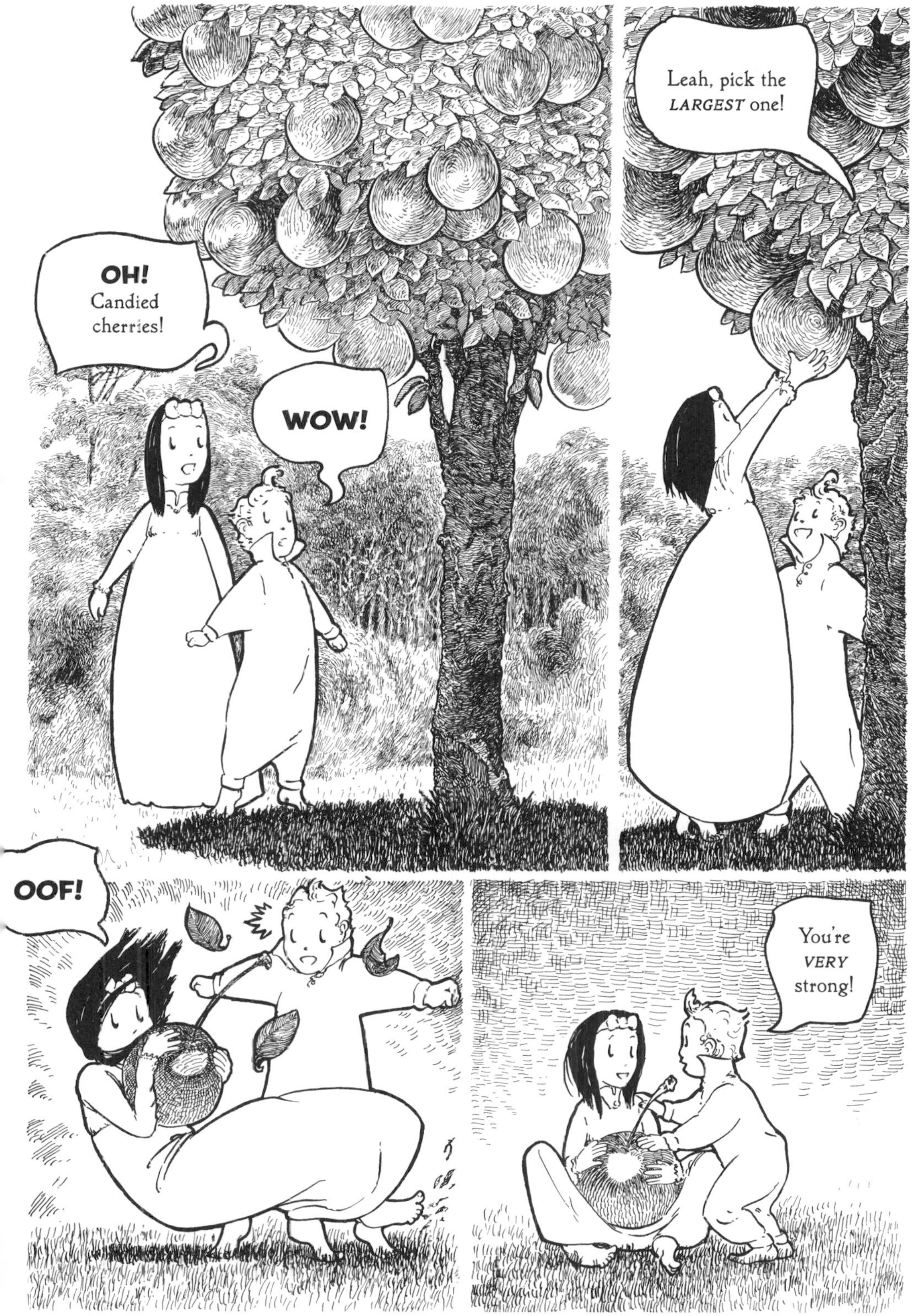
OH!
Candied cherries!
WOW!
Leah, pick the *LARGEST* one!
OOF!
You're *VERY* strong!

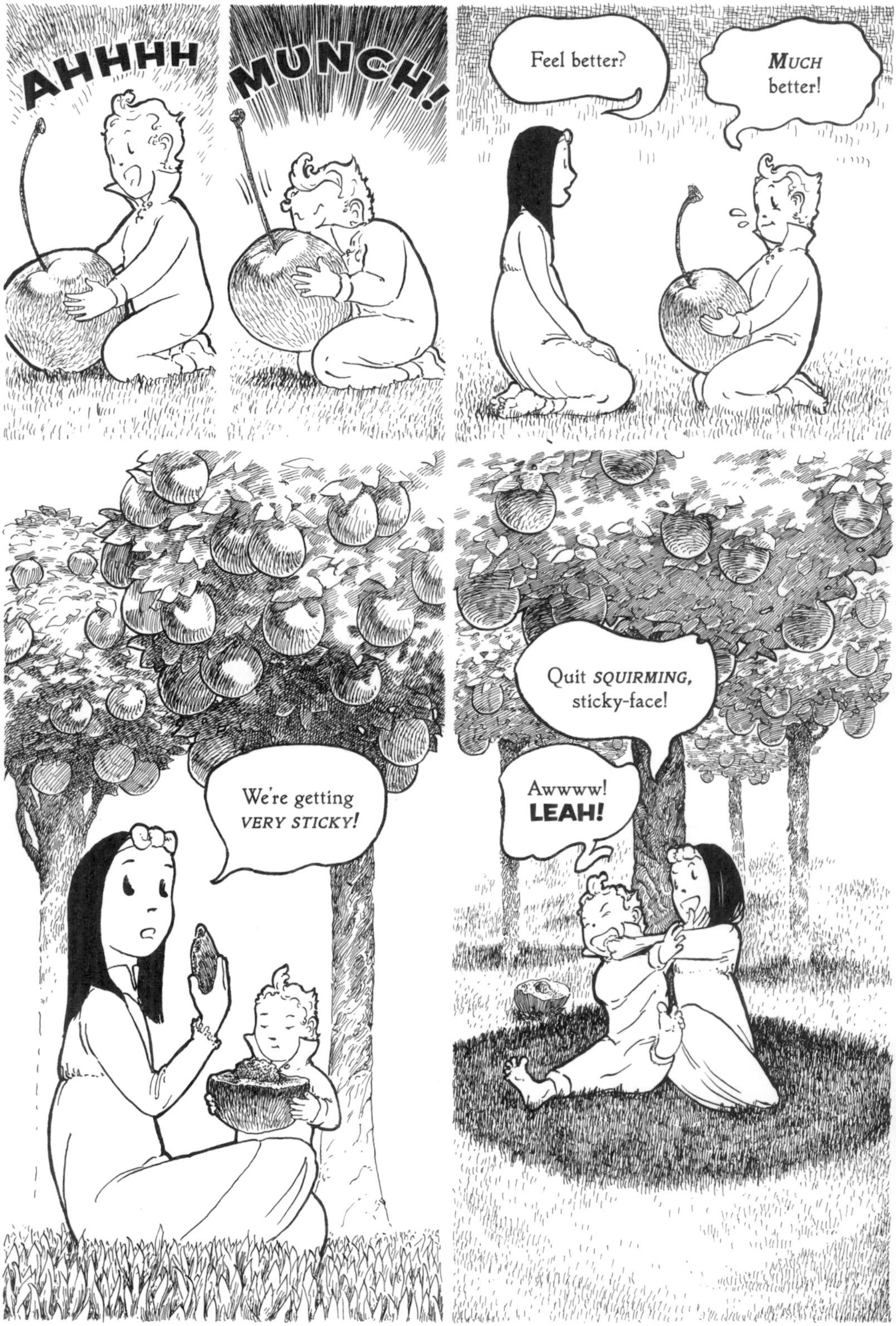
AHHHH
MUNCH!
Feel better?
MUCH better!
We're getting VERY STICKY!
Quit SQUIRMING, sticky-face!
Awwww! LEAH!

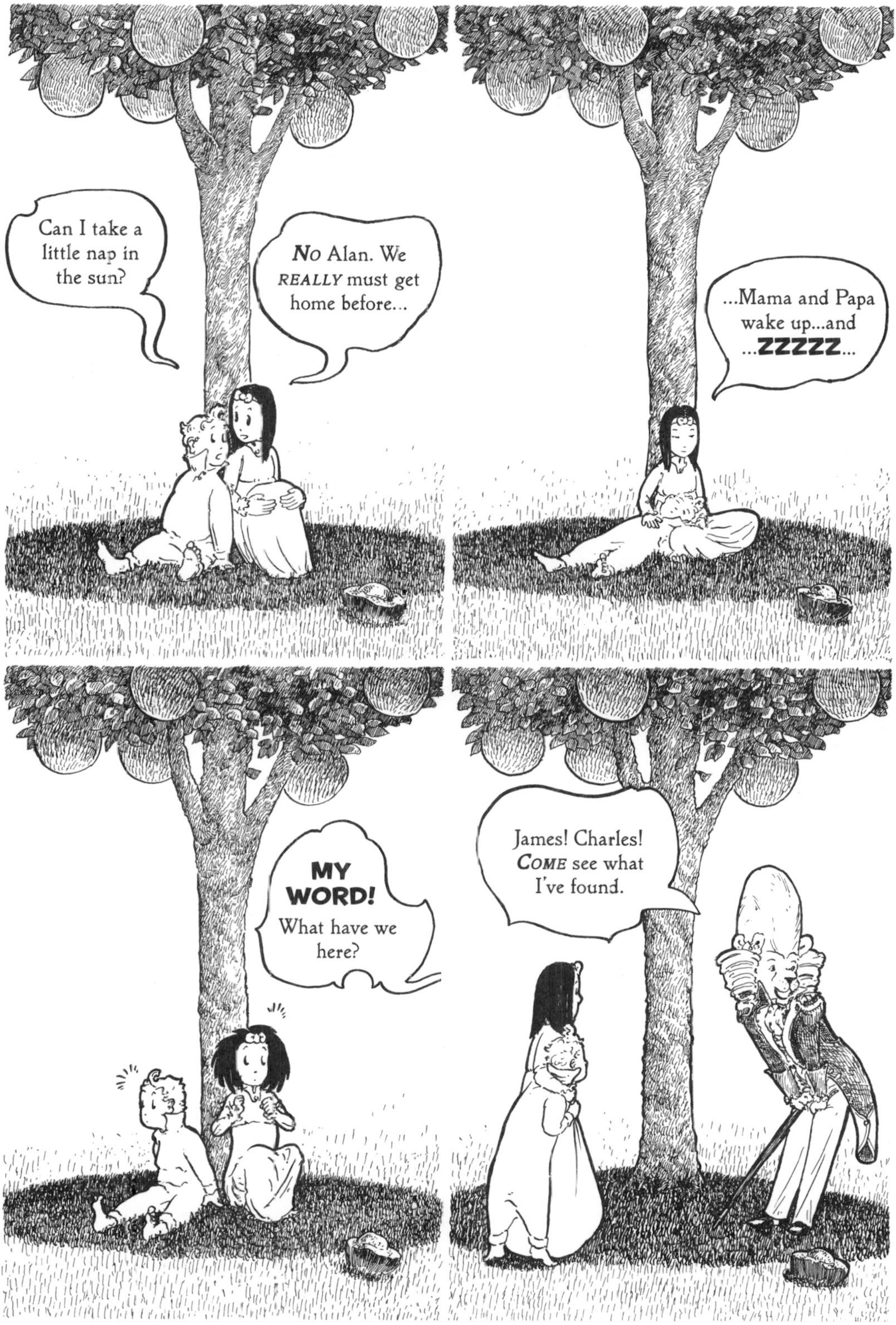
Can I take a little nap in the sun?
No Alan. We *REALLY* must get home before...
...Mama and Papa wake up...and ...**ZZZZZ**...
MY WORD! What have we here?
James! Charles! *COME* see what I've found.

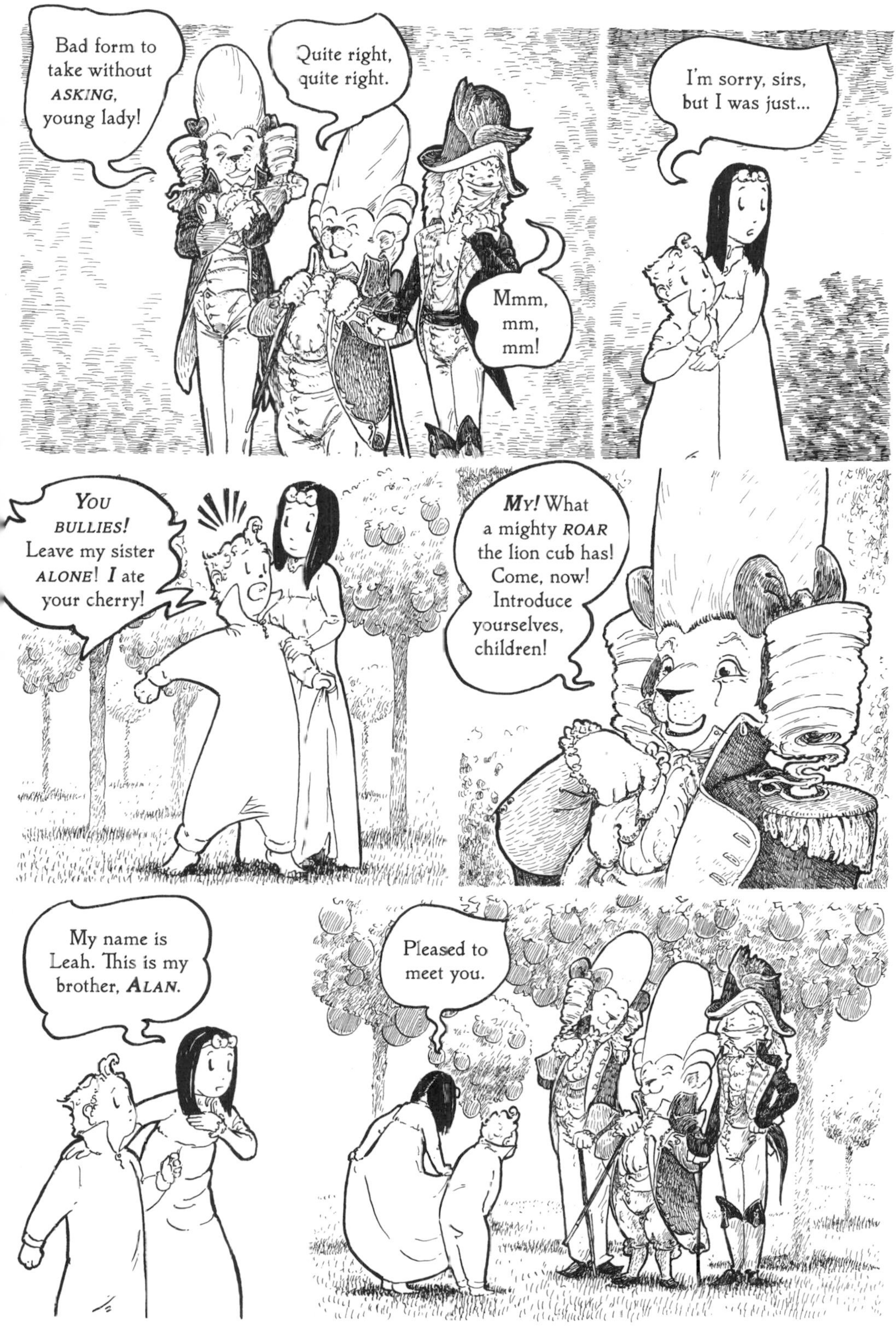
Bad form to take without ASKING, young lady!
Quite right, quite right.
Mmm, mm, mm!
I'm sorry, sirs, but I was just...
YOU BULLIES! Leave my sister ALONE! I ate your cherry!
MY! What a mighty ROAR the lion cub has! Come, now! Introduce yourselves, children!
My name is Leah. This is my brother, ALAN.
Pleased to meet you.

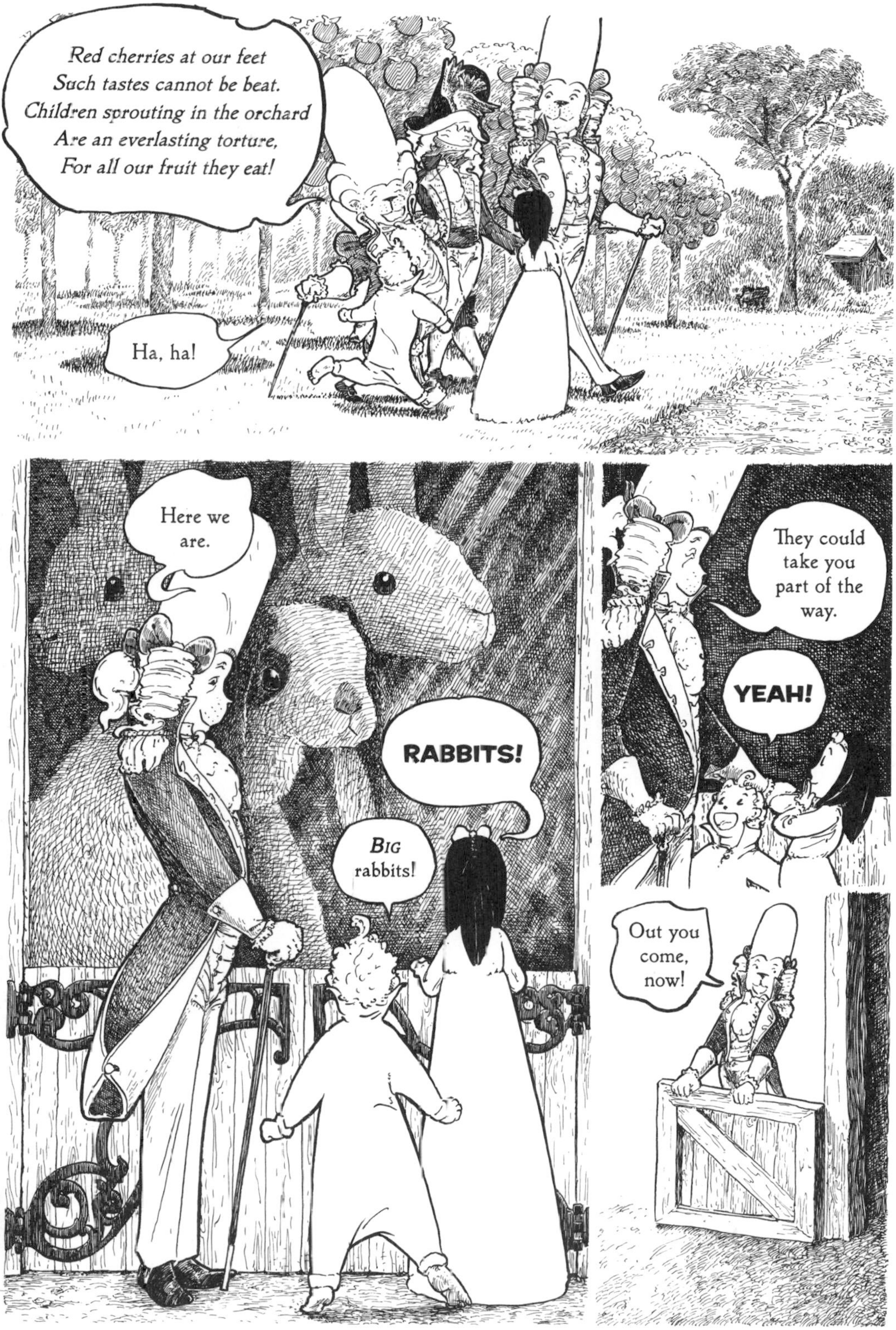
Red cherries at our feet
Such tastes cannot be beat.
Children sprouting in the orchard
Are an everlasting torture,
For all our fruit they eat!
Ha, ha!
Here we are.
RABBITS!
BIG rabbits!
They could take you part of the way.
YEAH!
Out you come, now!

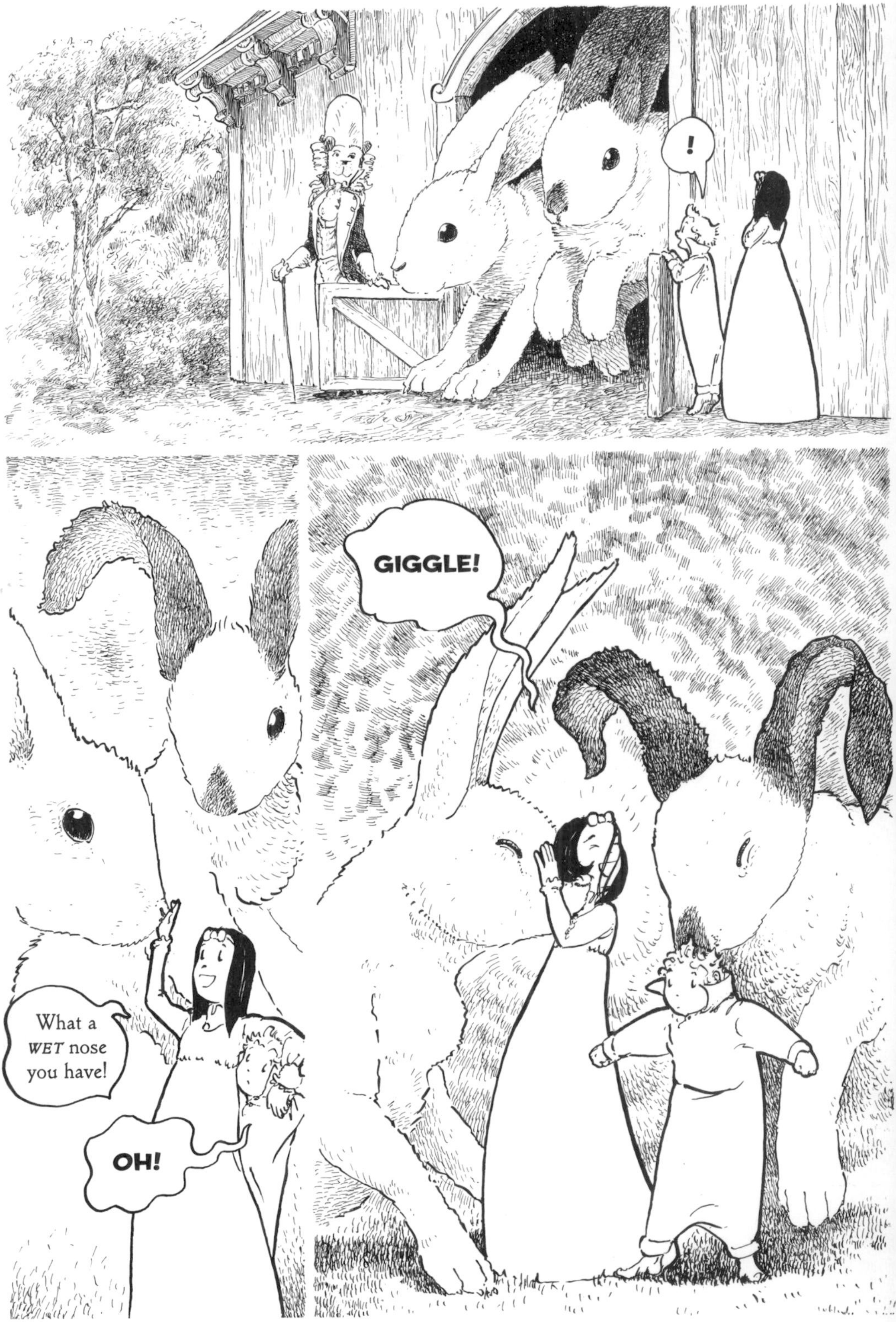
!
What a WET nose you have!
OH!
GIGGLE!

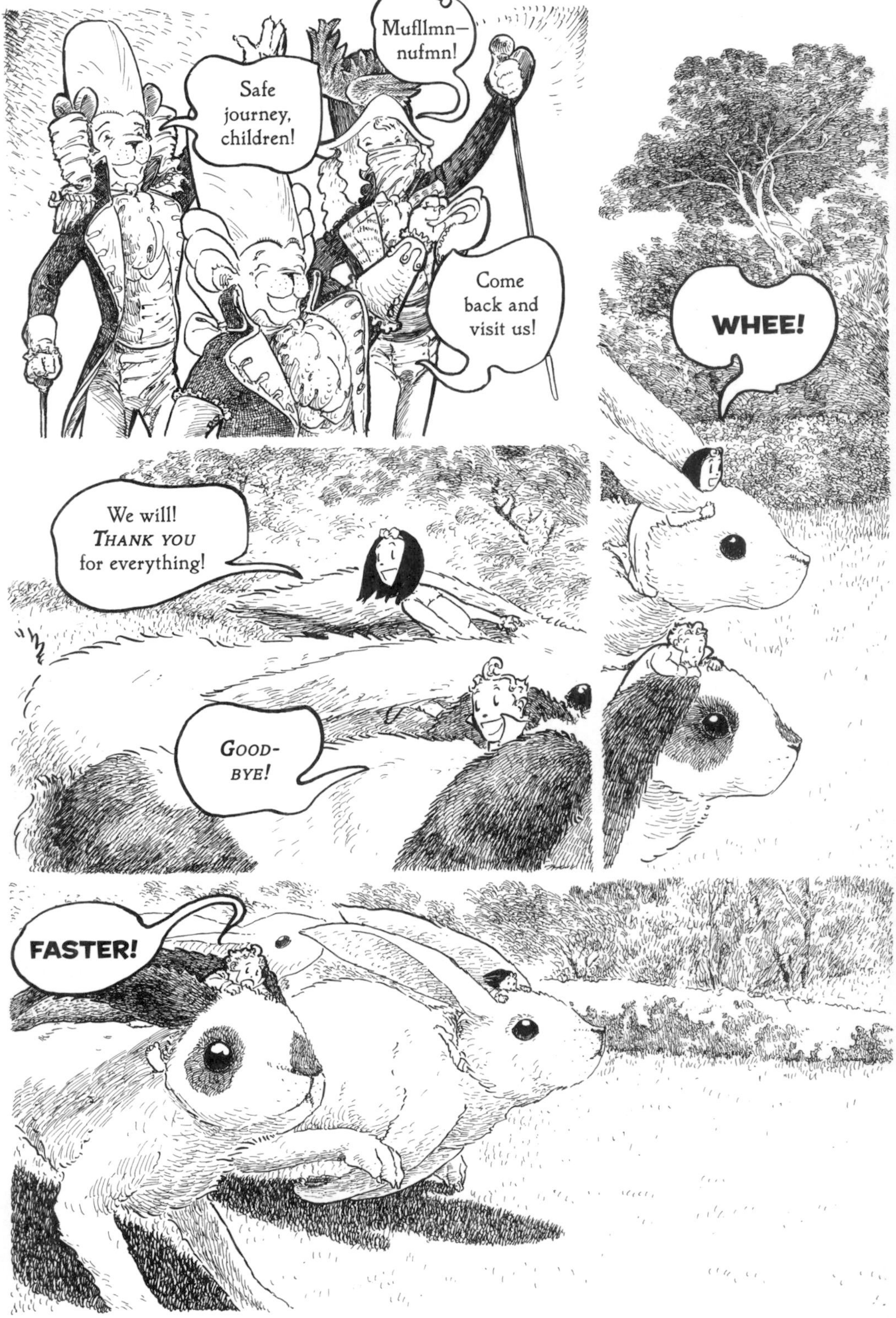
Mufllmn—nufmn!
Safe journey, children!
Come back and visit us!
WHEE!
We will! THANK YOU for everything!
GOOD-BYE!
FASTER!

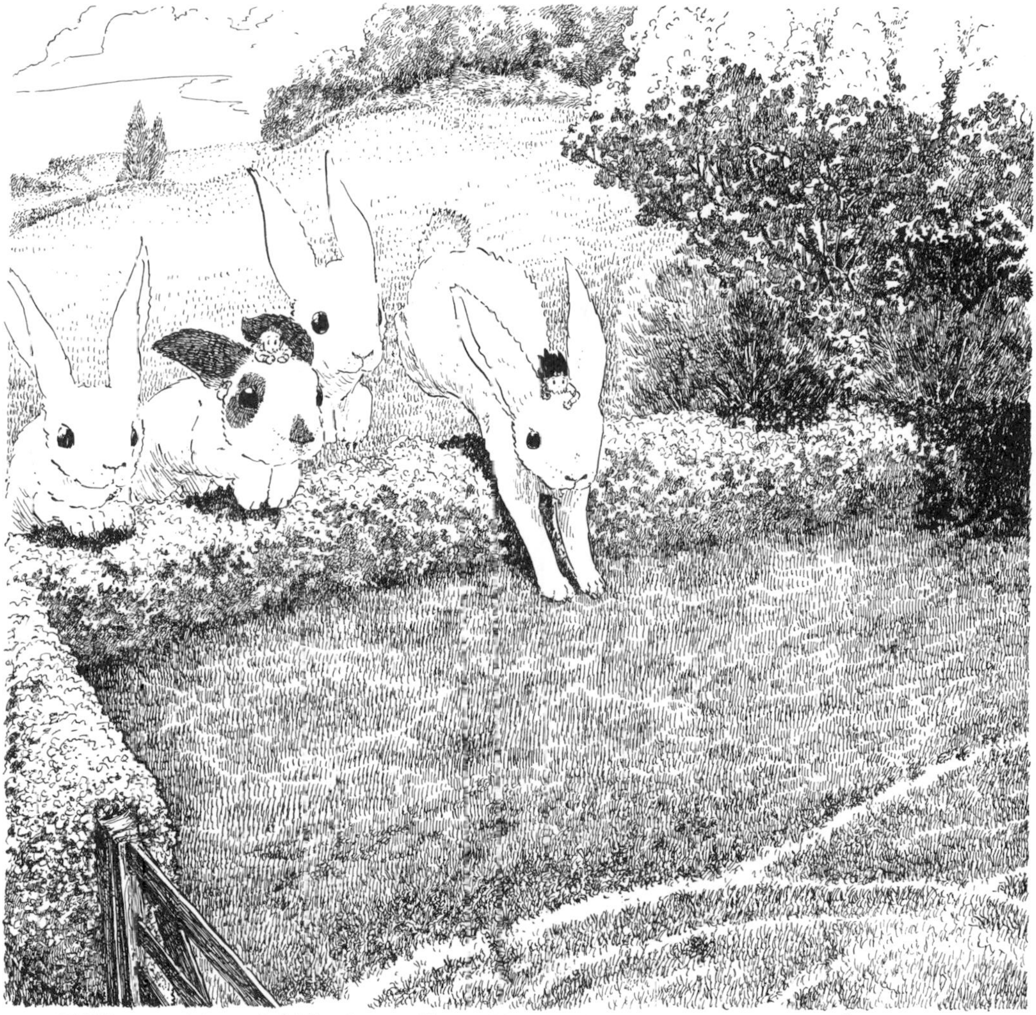

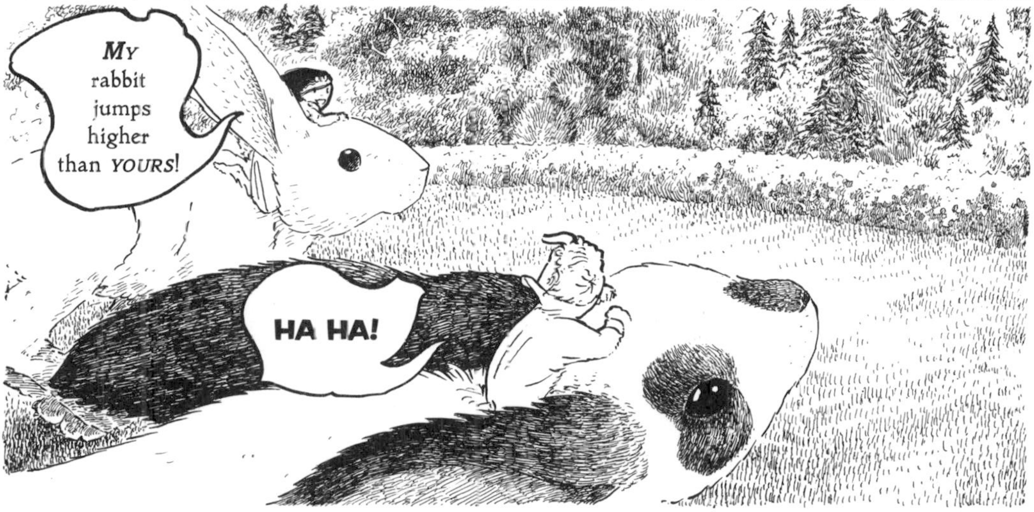
MY rabbit jumps higher than YOURS!
HA HA!

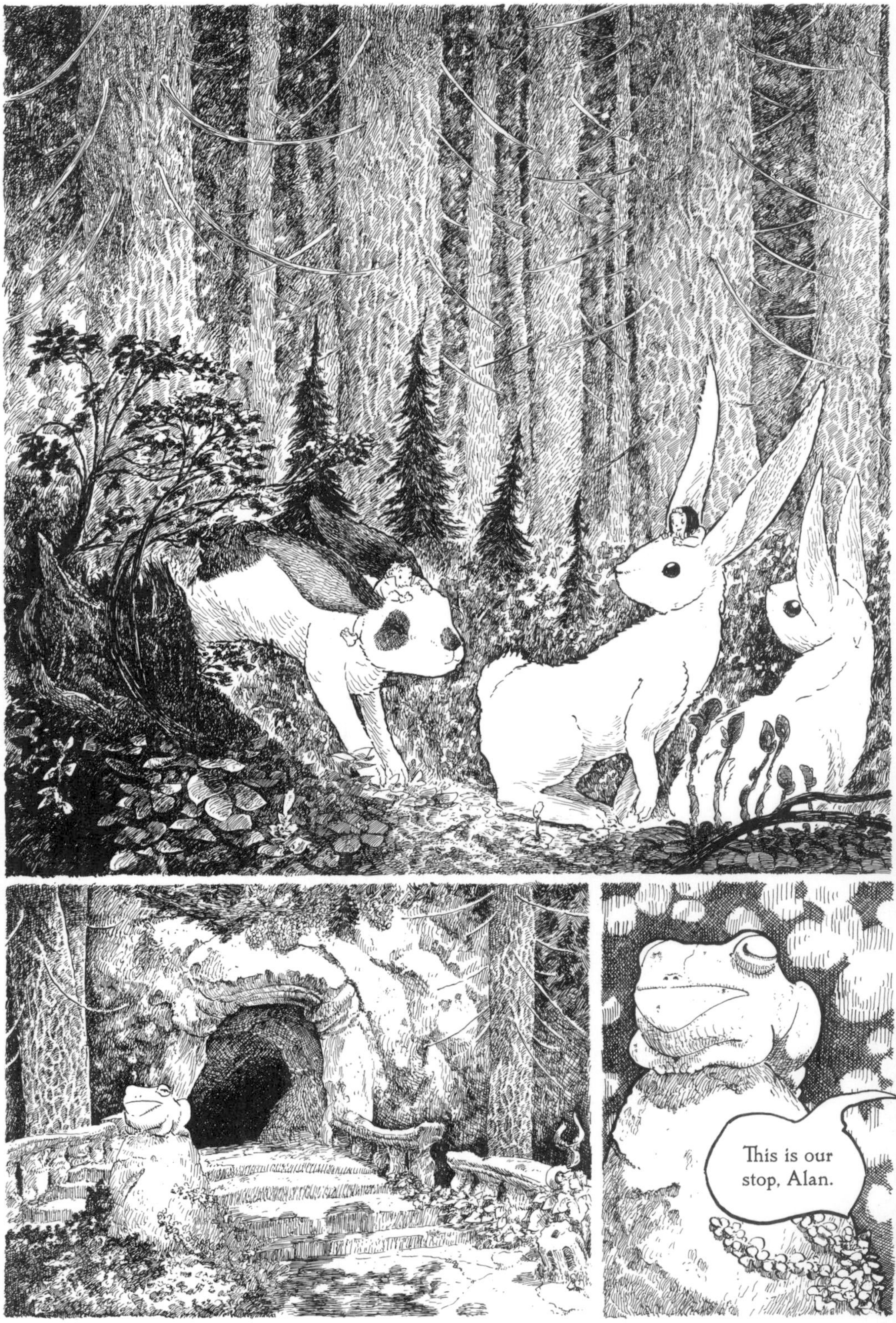
This is our stop, Alan.

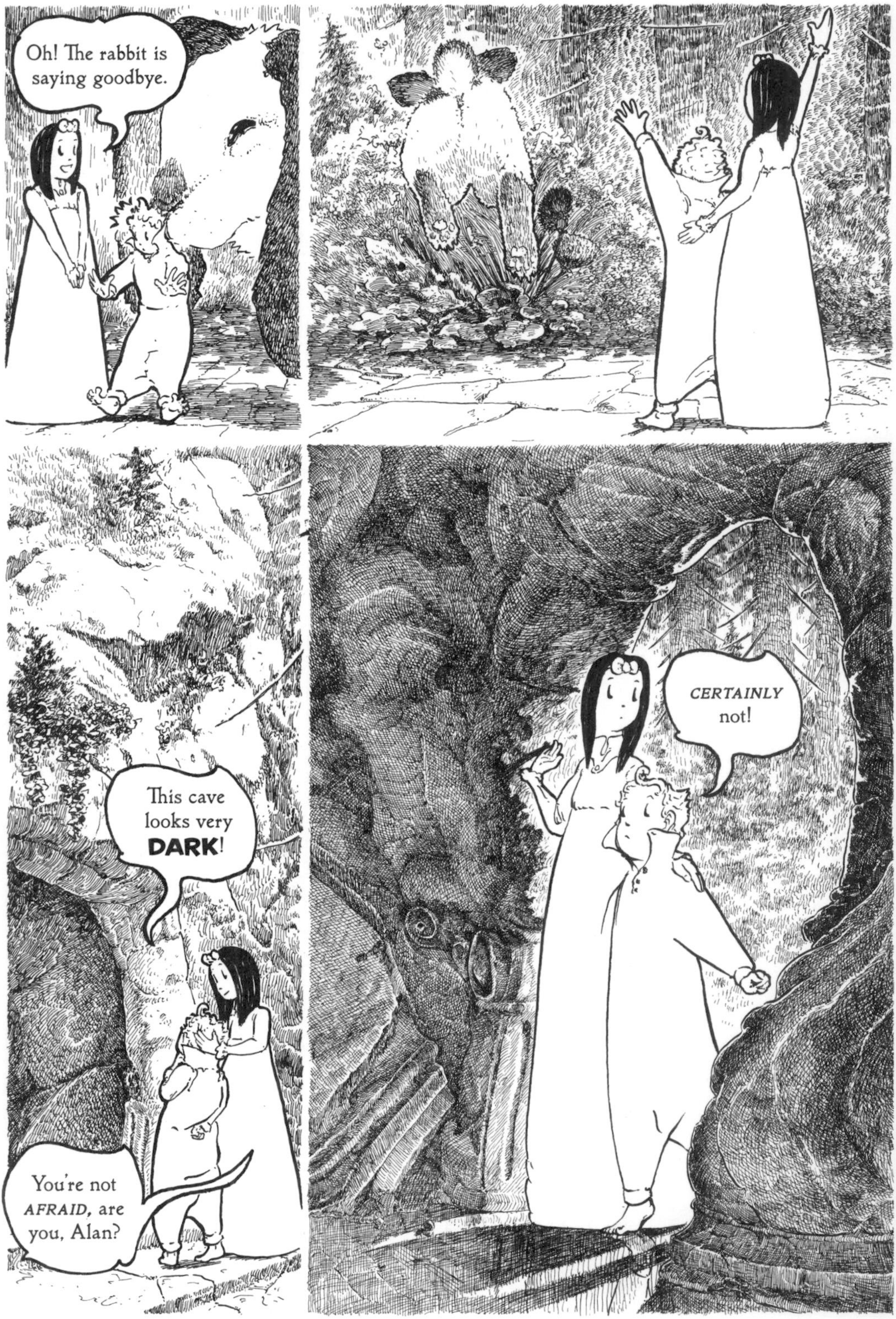
Oh! The rabbit is saying goodbye.
This cave looks very **DARK**!
You're not *AFRAID,* are you, Alan?
CERTAINLY not!

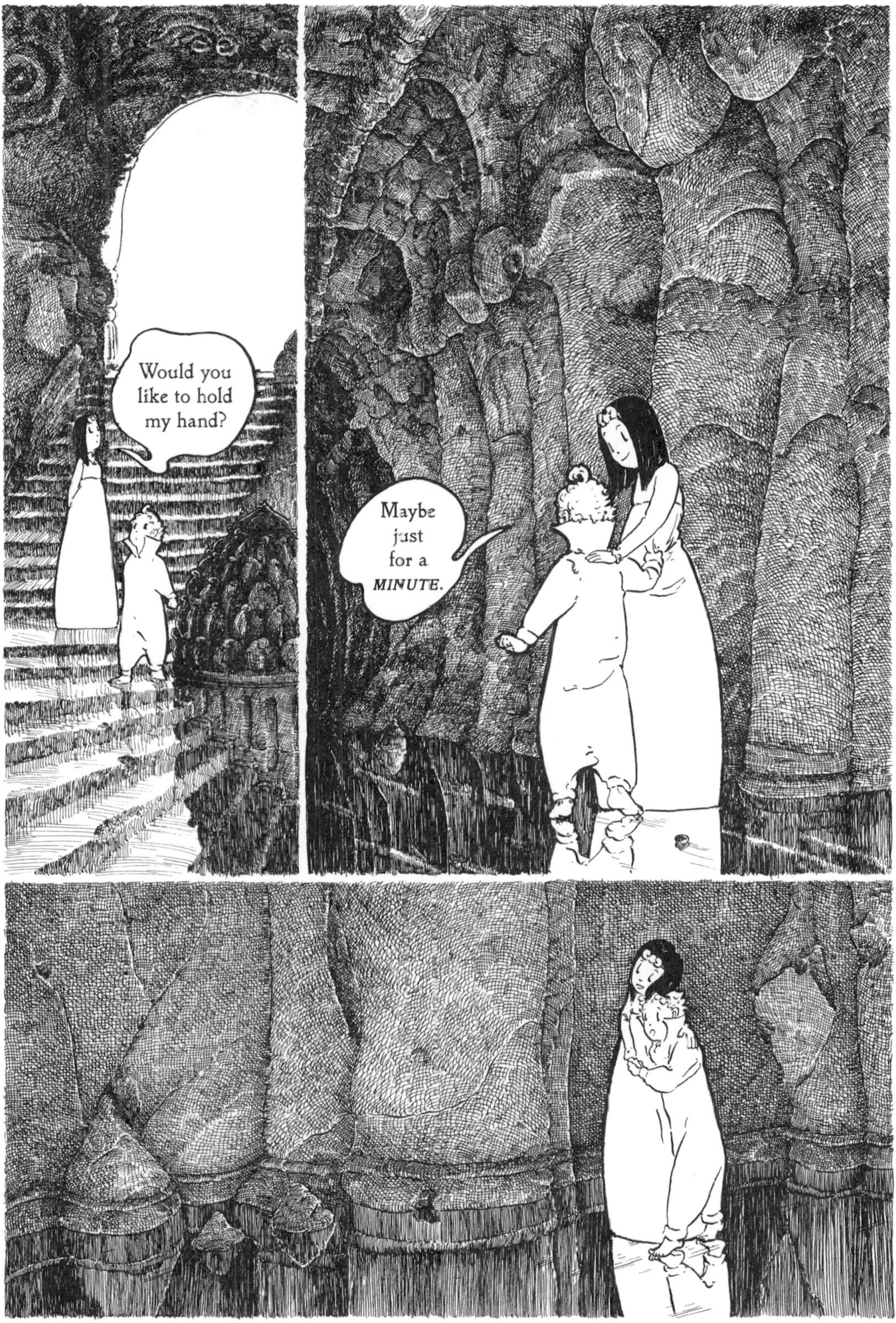
Would you like to hold my hand?
Maybe just for a *MINUTE.*

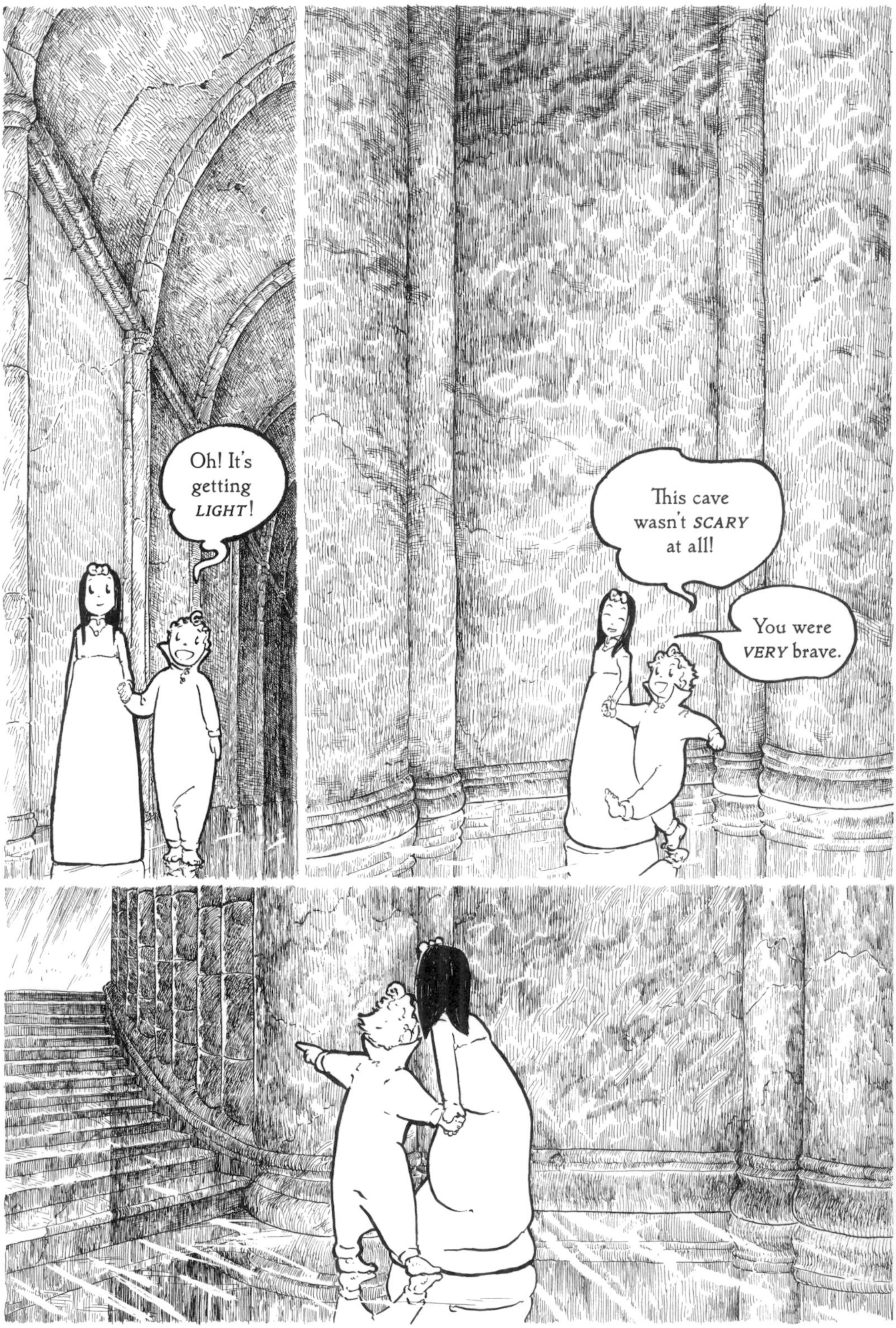
Oh! It's getting LIGHT!
This cave wasn't SCARY at all!
You were VERY brave.

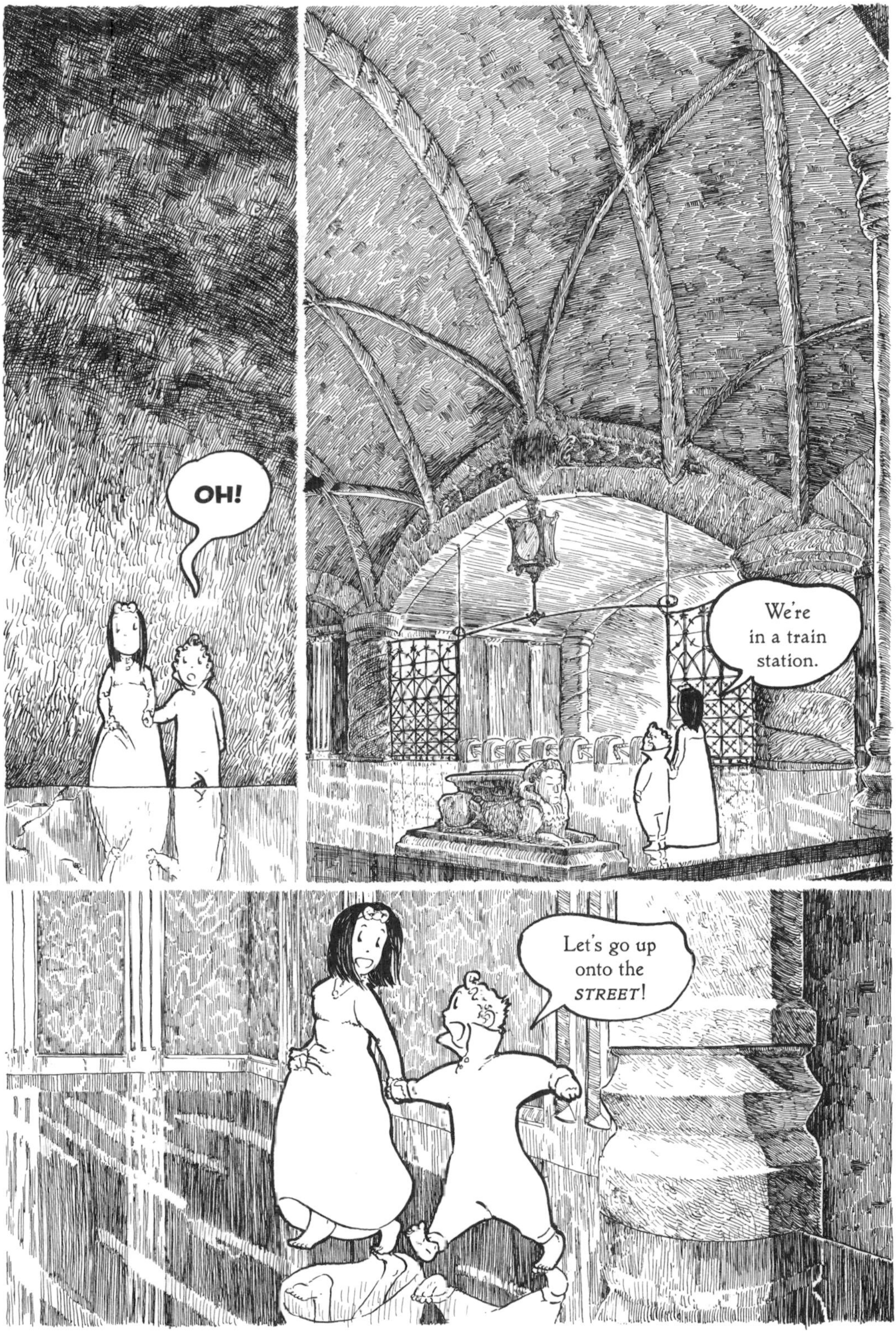
OH!
We're in a train station.
Let's go up onto the *STREET*!

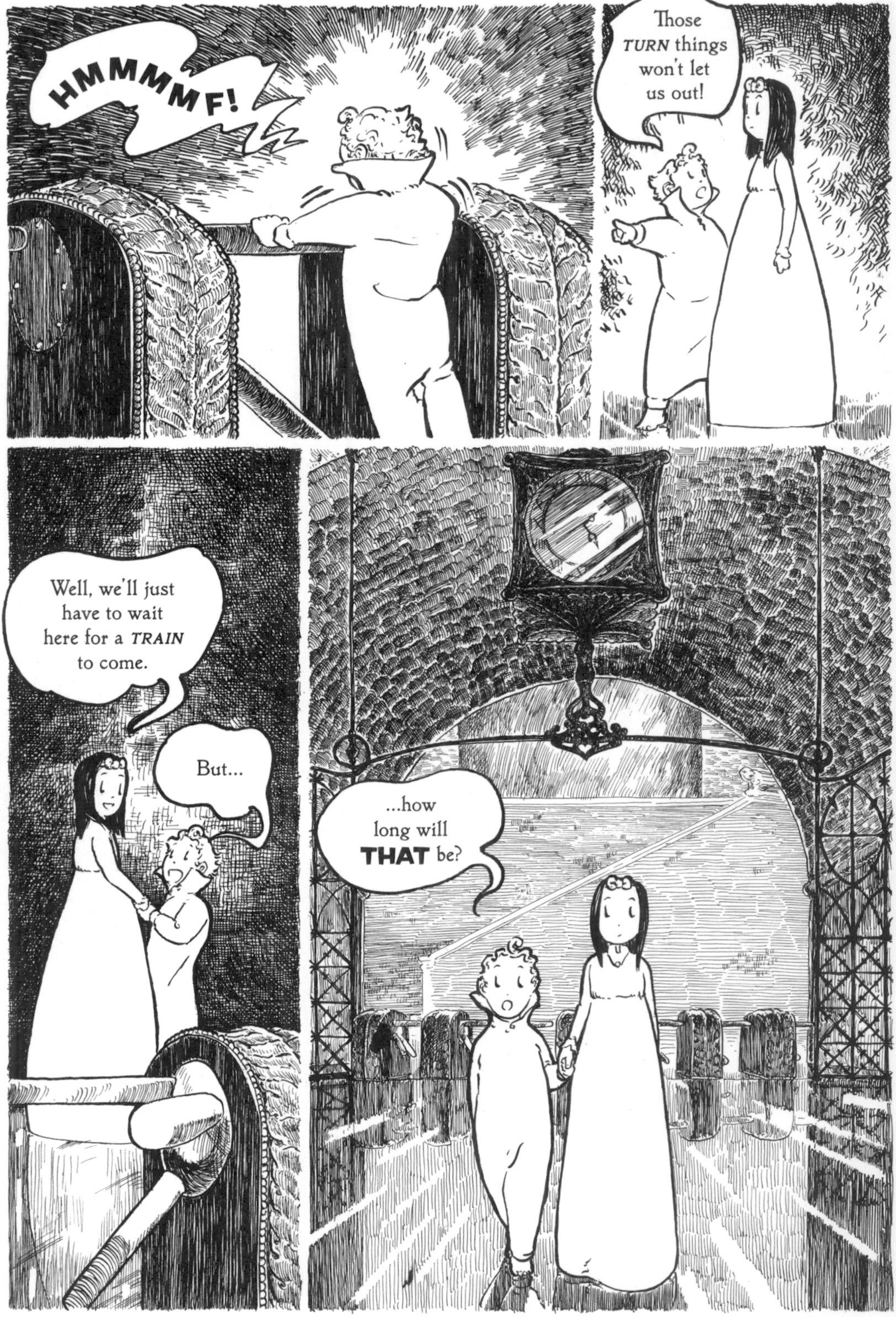
HMMMMF!
Those TURN things won't let us out!
Well, we'll just have to wait here for a TRAIN to come.
But...
...how long will THAT be?

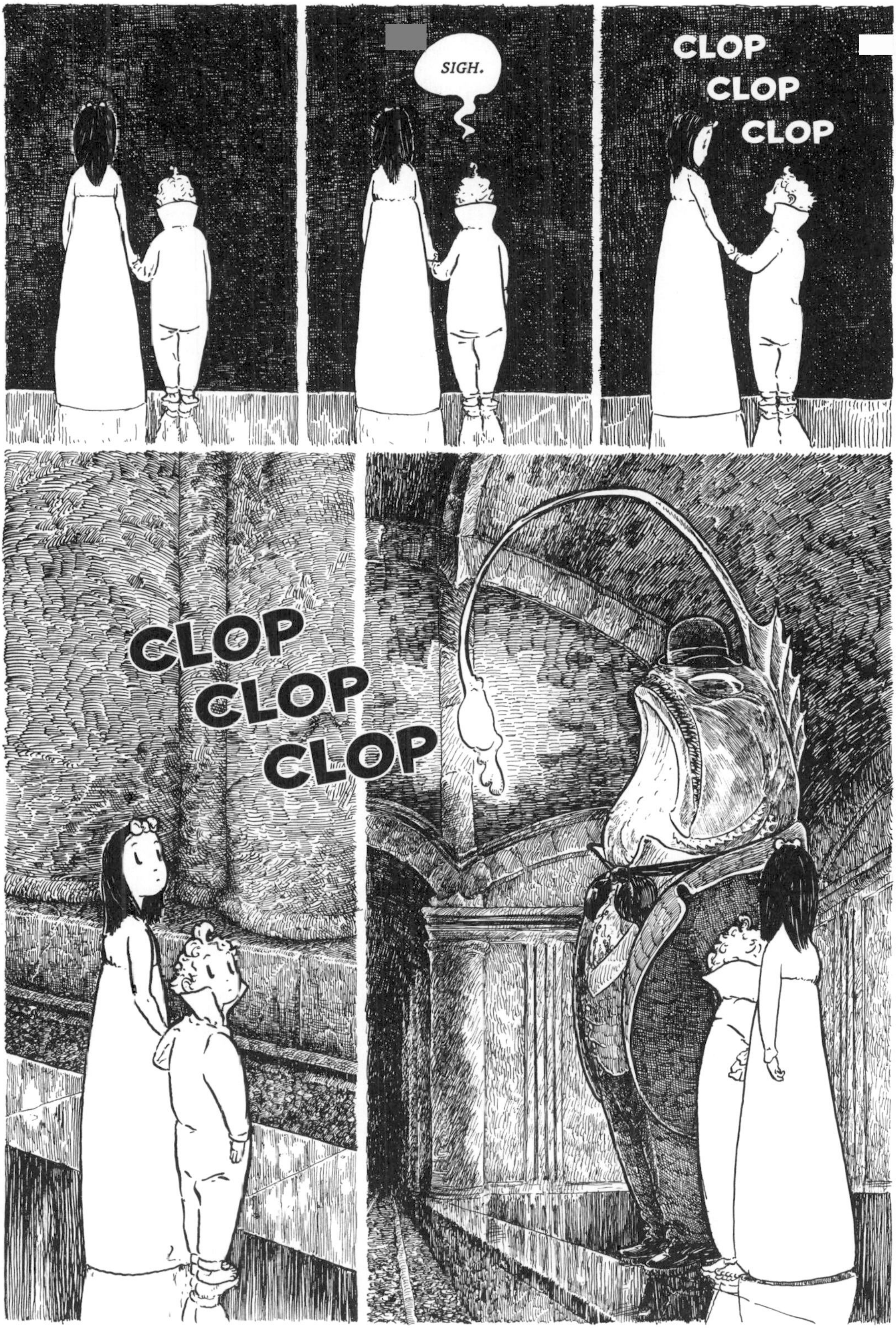
SIGH.
CLOP
CLOP
CLOP
CLOP
CLOP
CLOP

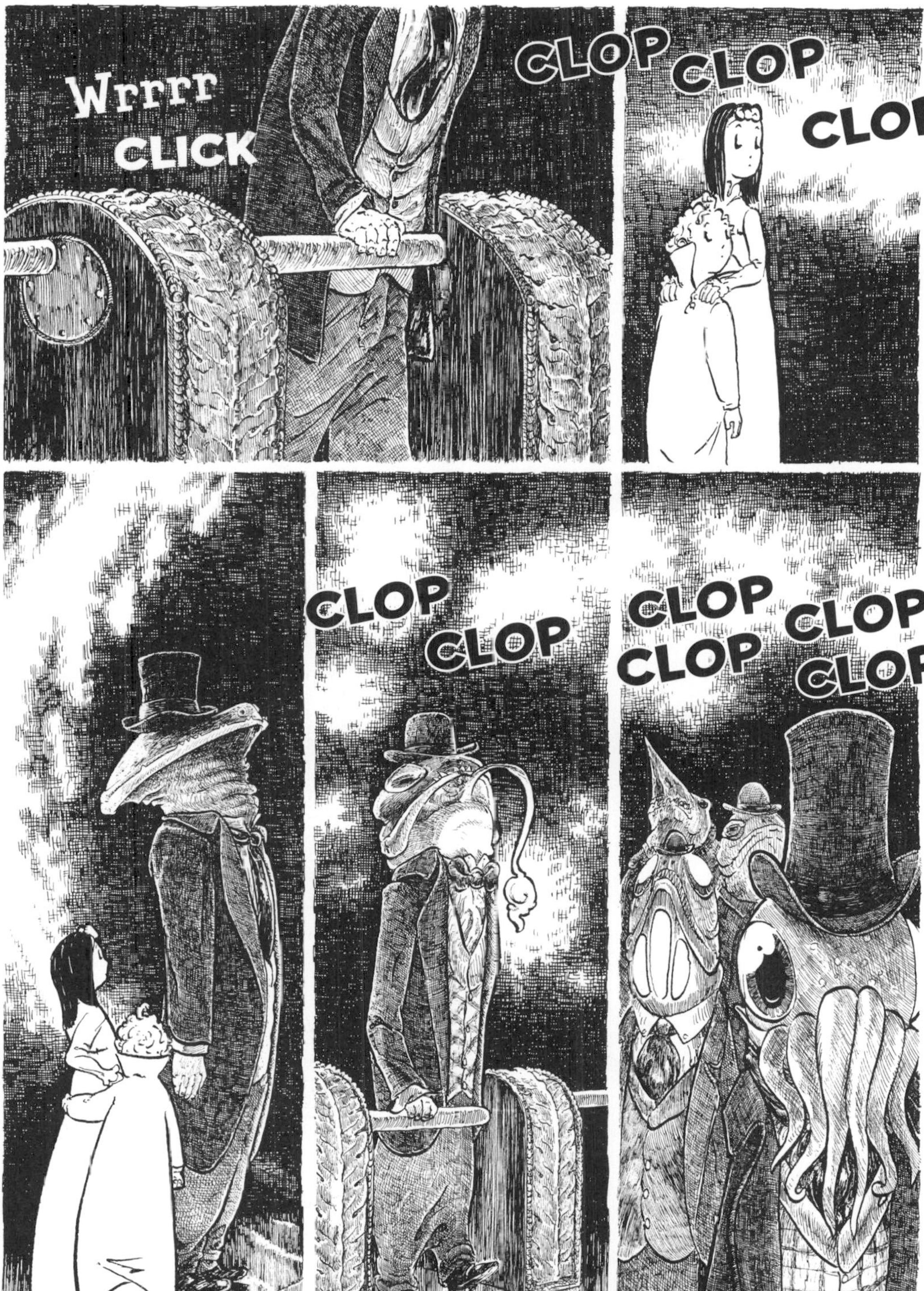
Wrrrr
CLICK
CLOP
CLOP
CLOP
CLOP
CLOP
CLOP
CLOP
CLOP
CLOP

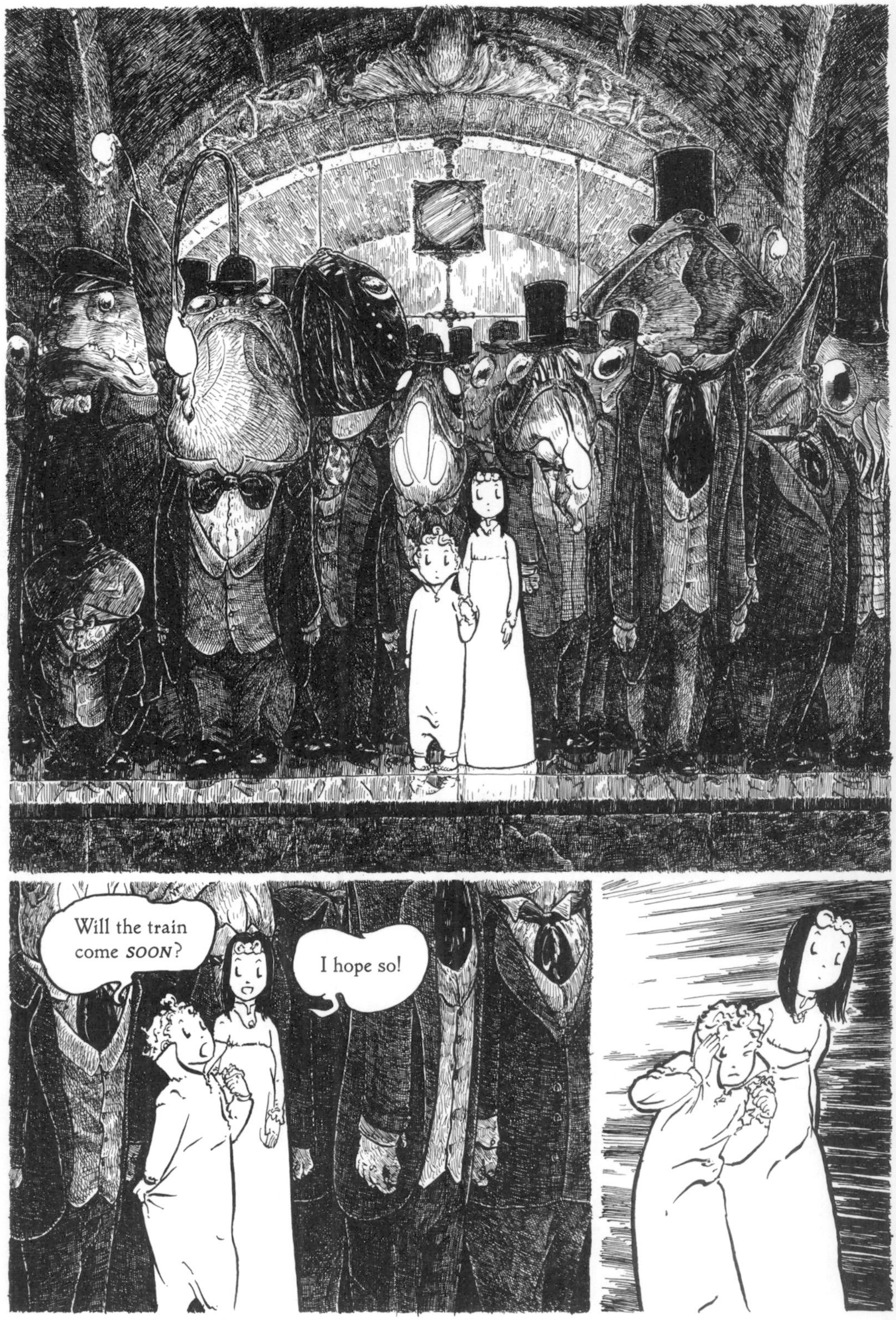

Will the train come SOON?
I hope so!

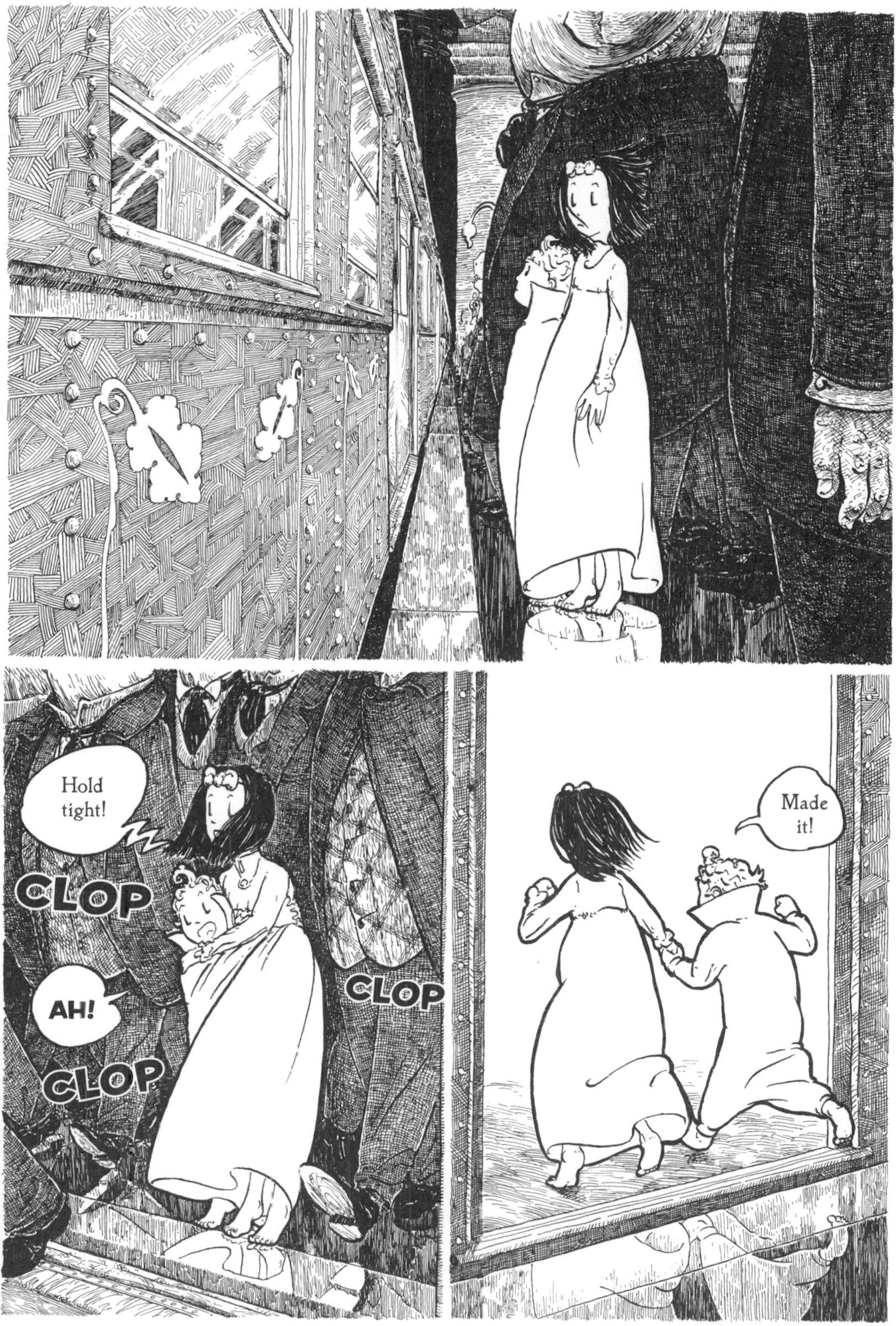

Hold tight!
CLOP
AH!
CLOP
CLOP
Made it!

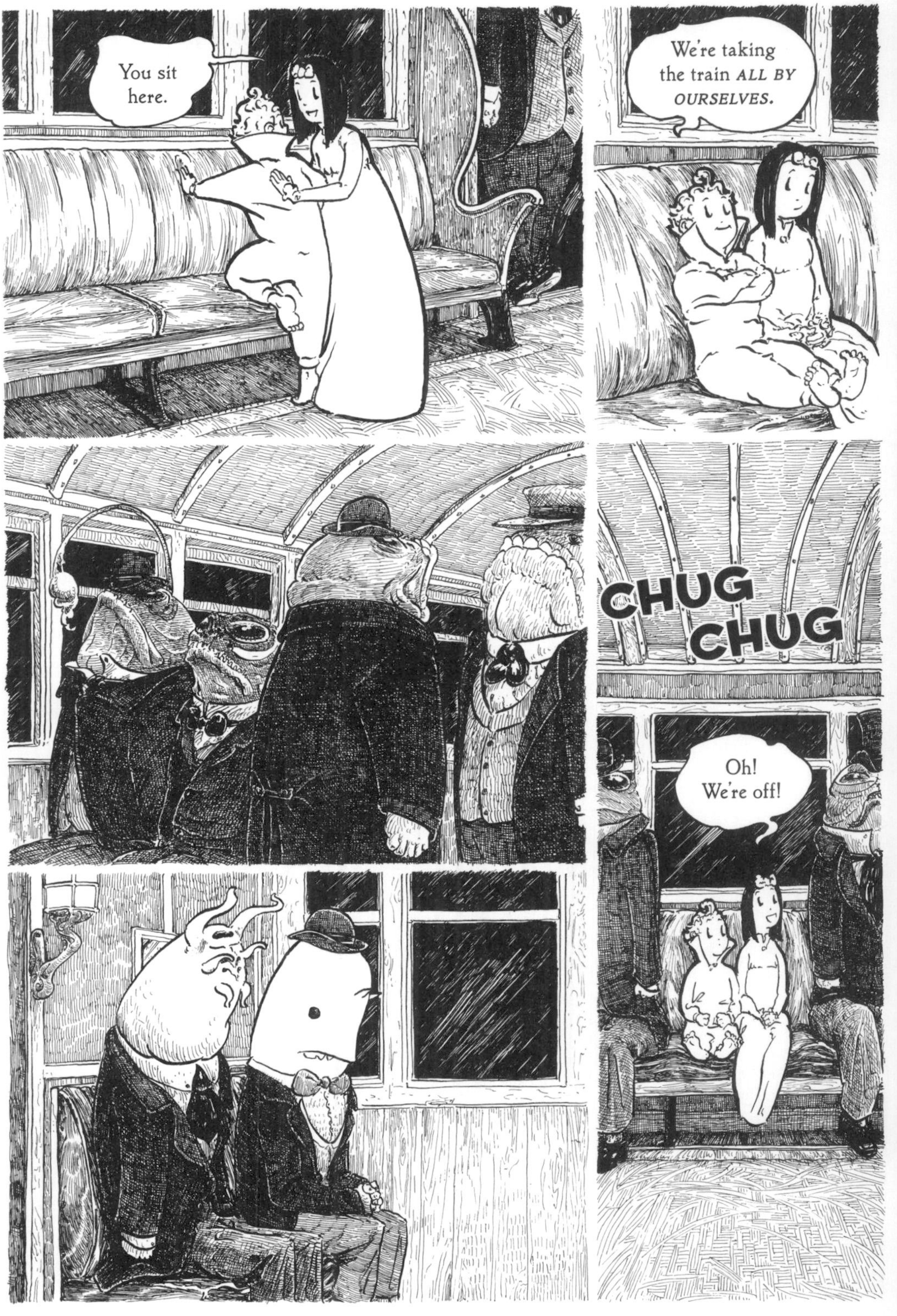
You sit here.
We're taking the train ALL BY OURSELVES.
CHUG CHUG
Oh! We're off!

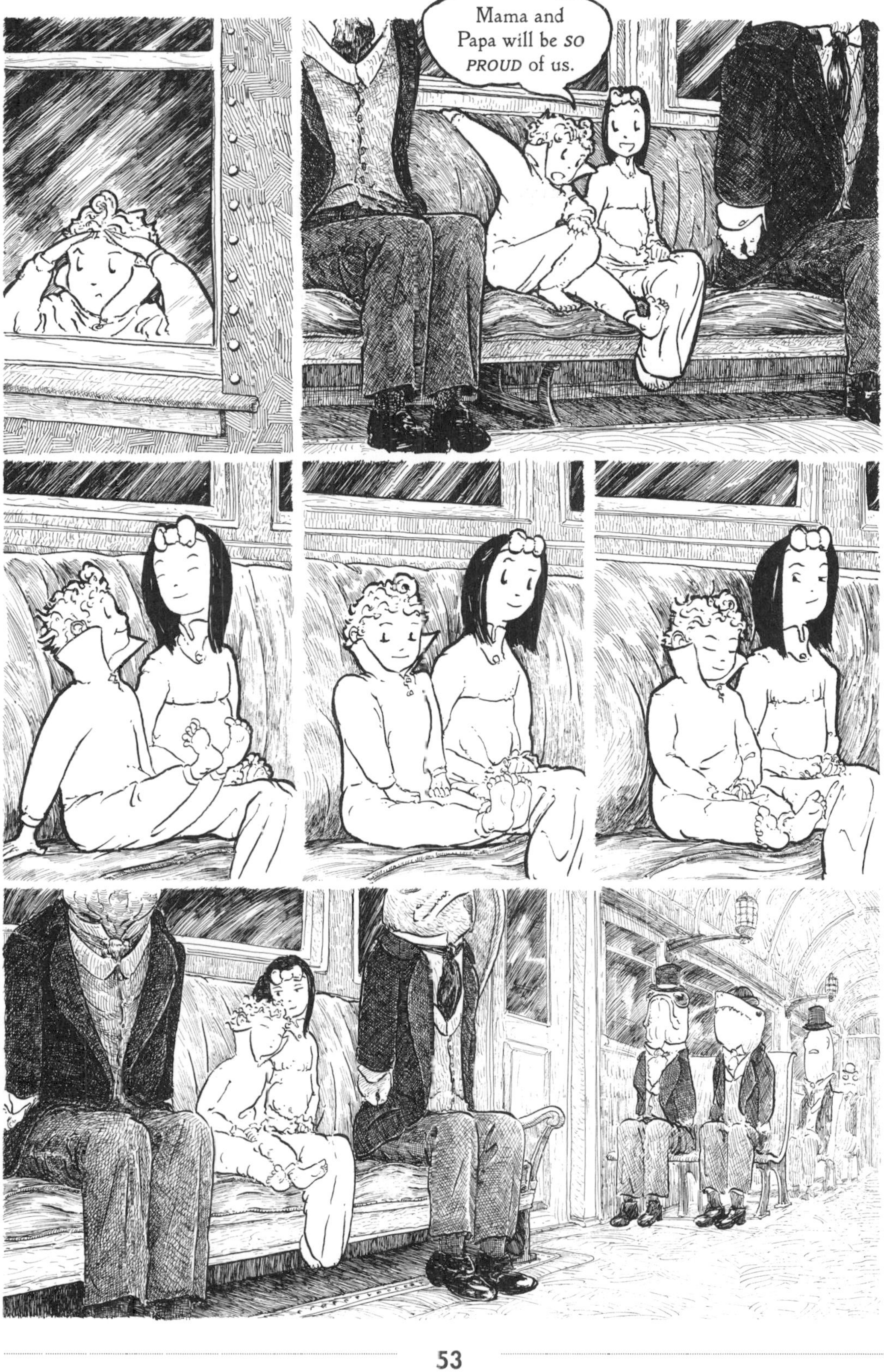

Mama and Papa will be *SO PROUD* of us.

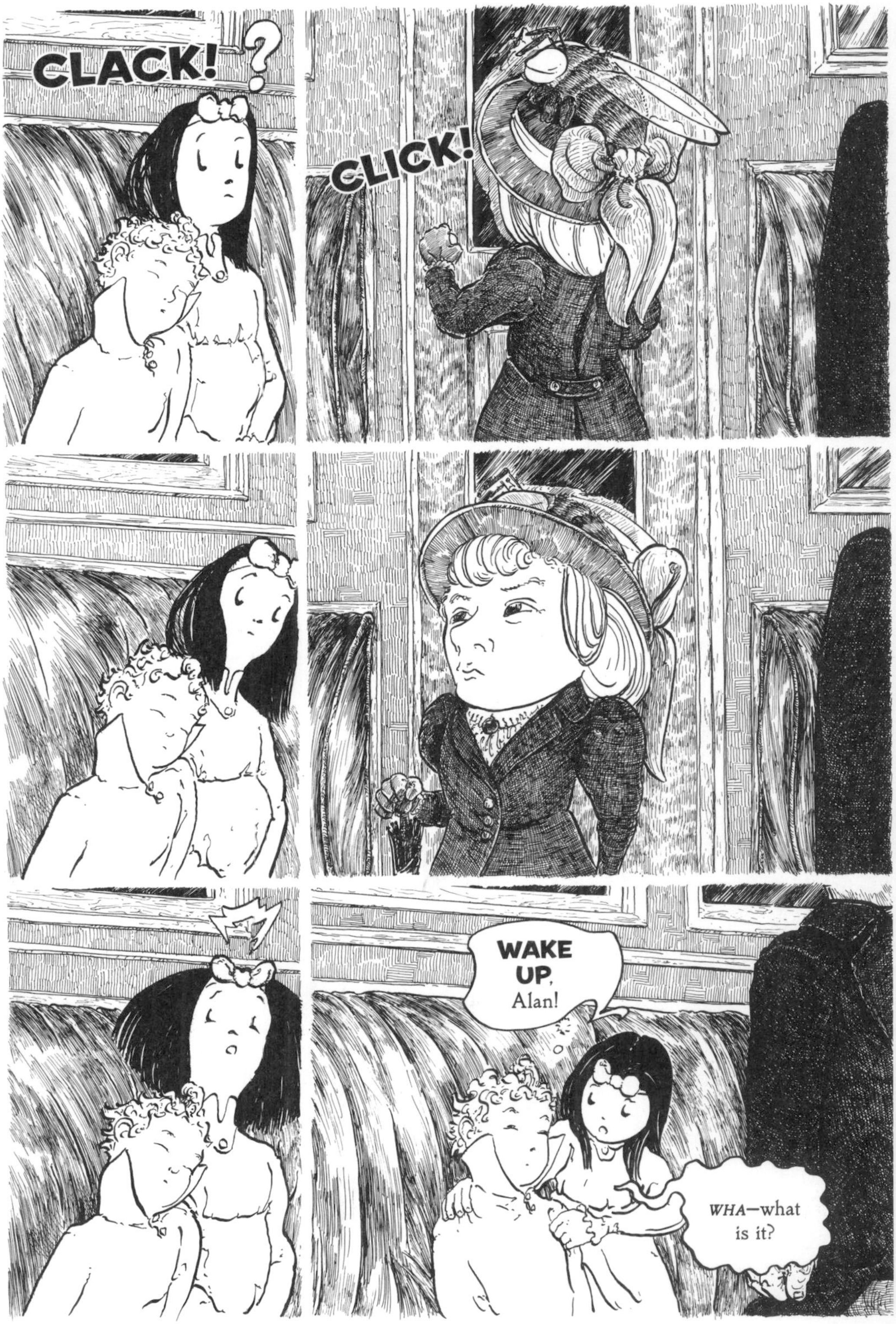
CLACK!
CLICK!
WAKE UP, Alan!
WHA—what is it?

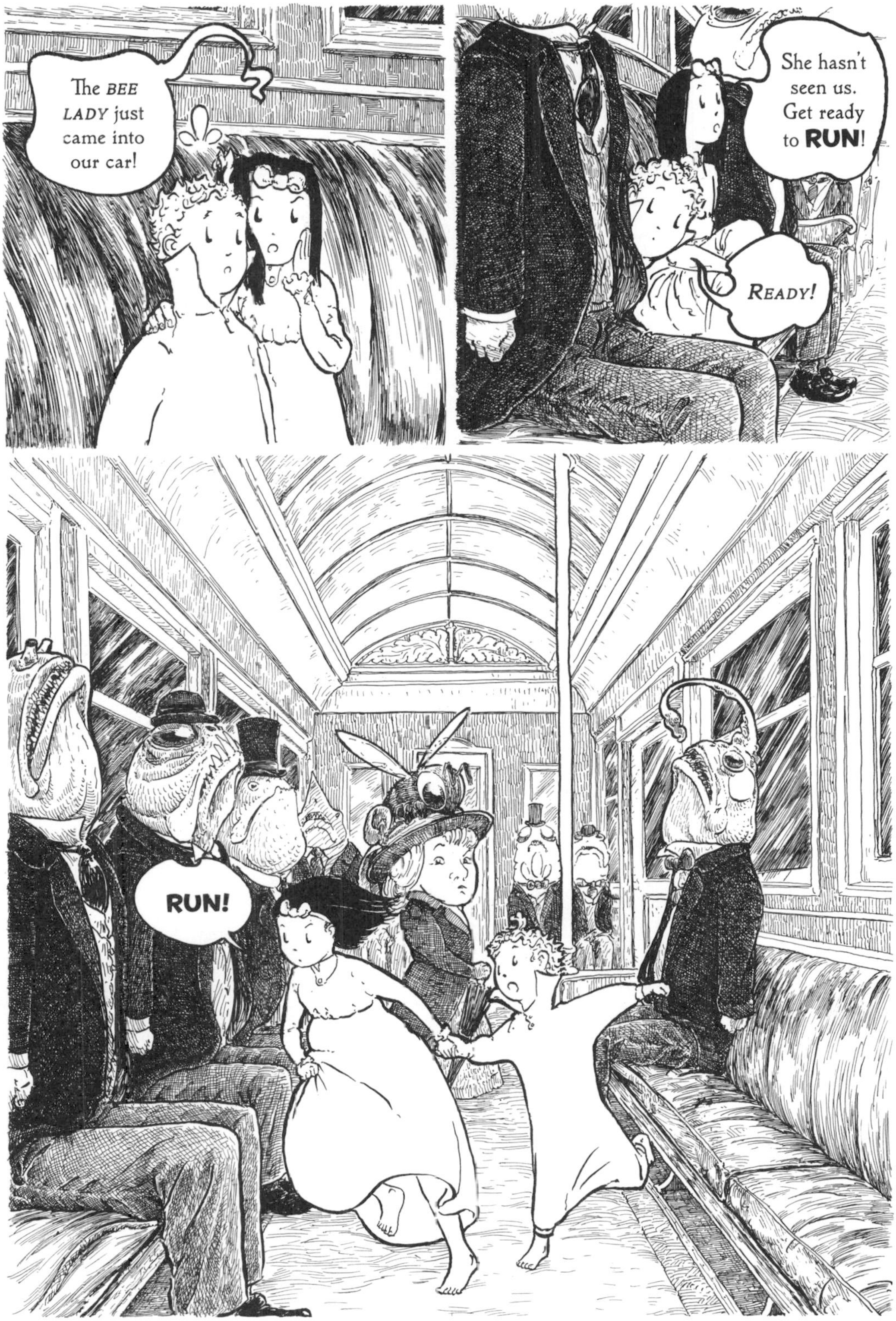
The BEE LADY just came into our car!
She hasn't seen us. Get ready to RUN!
READY!
RUN!

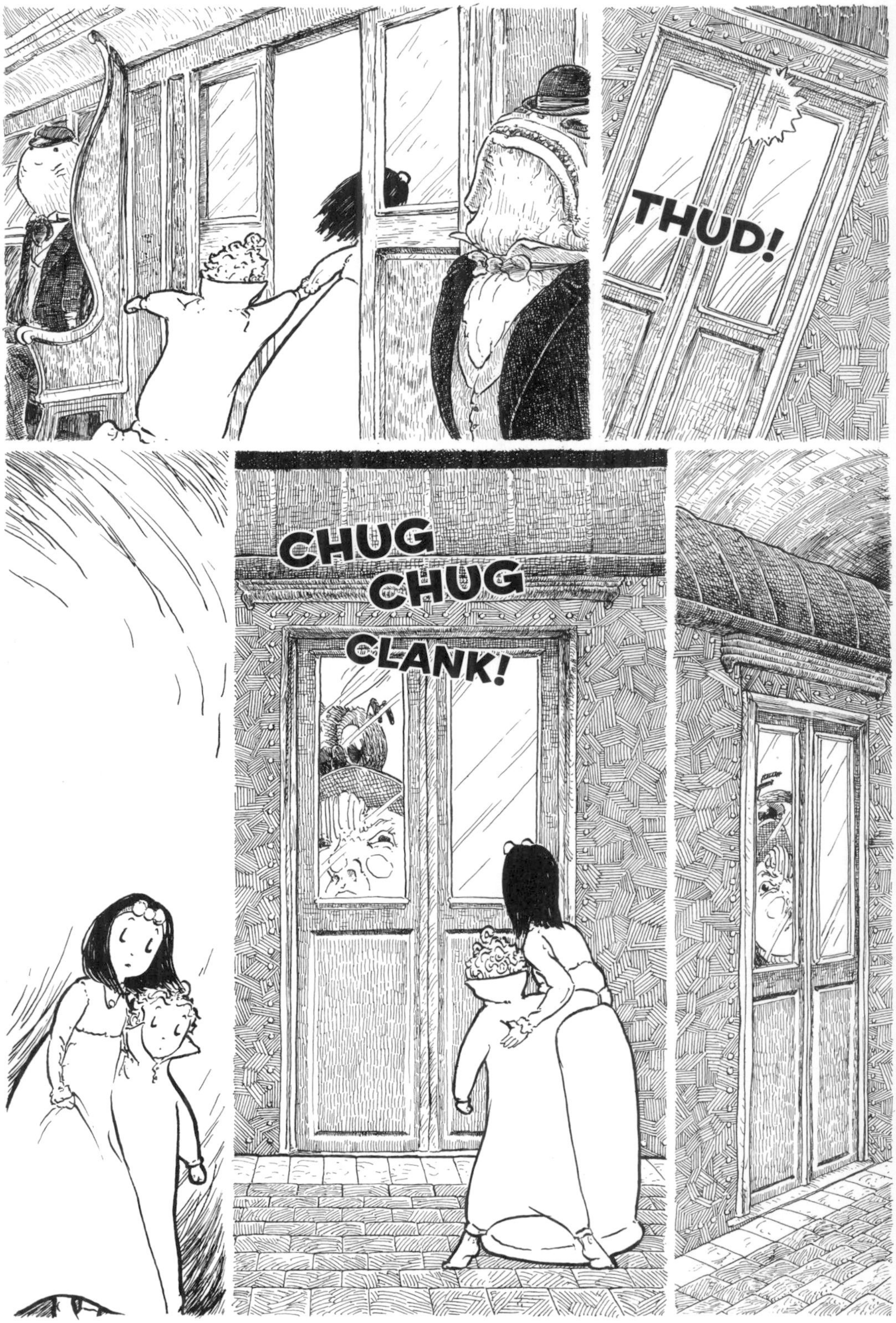
THUD!
CHUG
CHUG
CLANK!

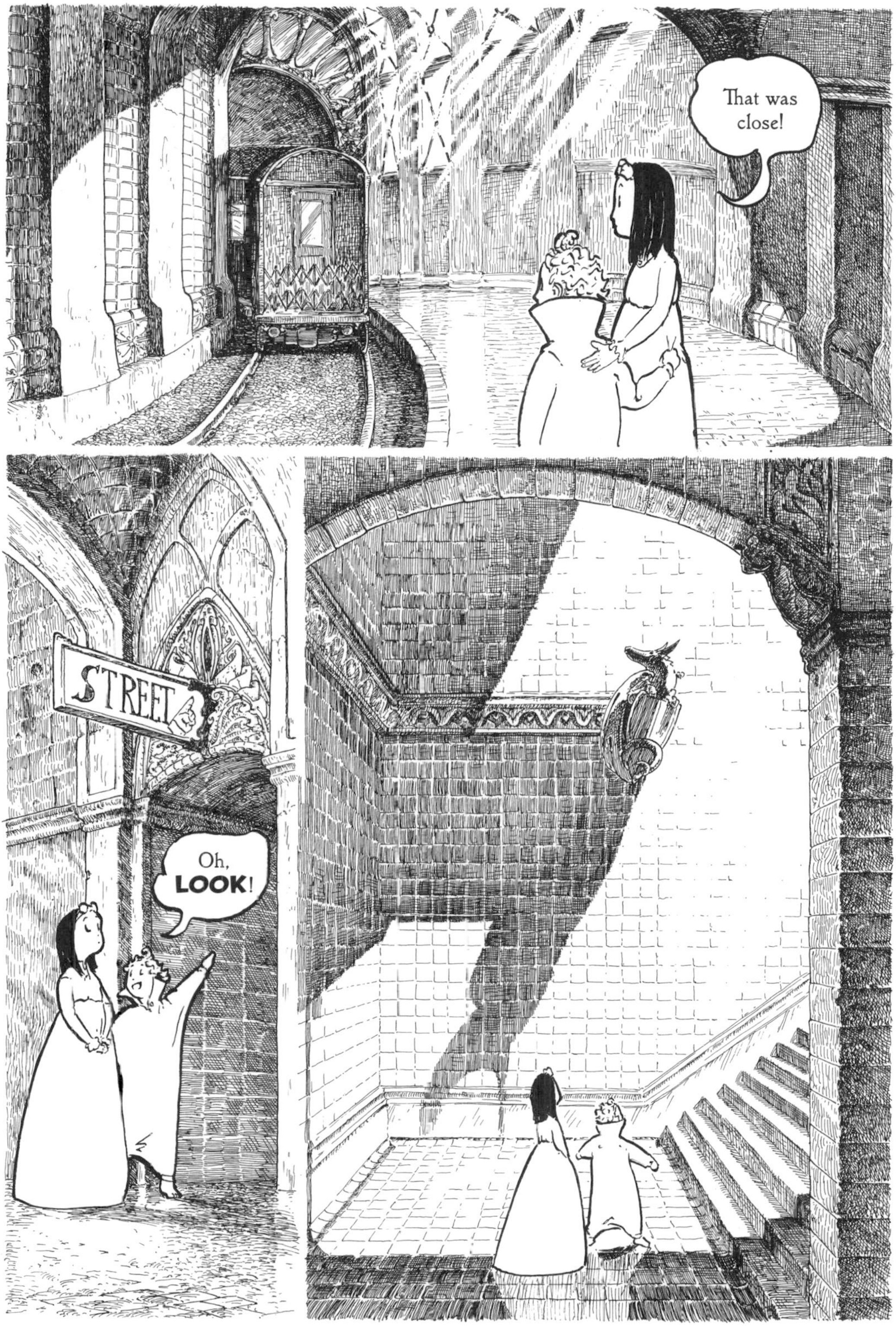
That was close!
STREET
Oh, LOOK!

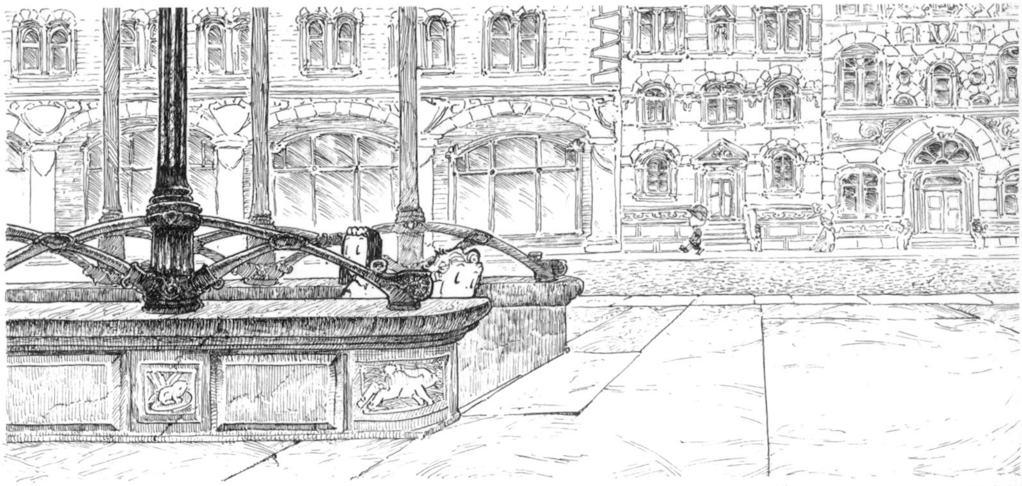

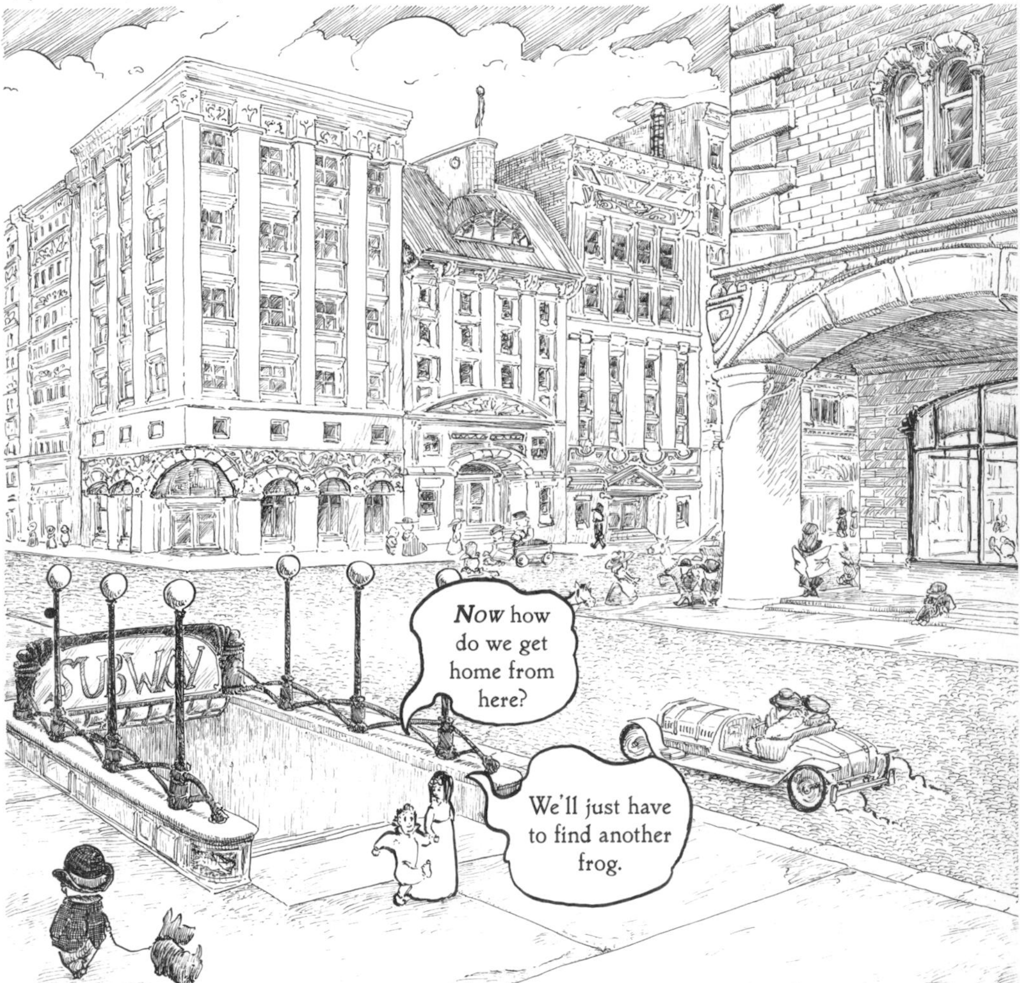
SUBWAY
Now how do we get home from here?
We'll just have to find another frog.

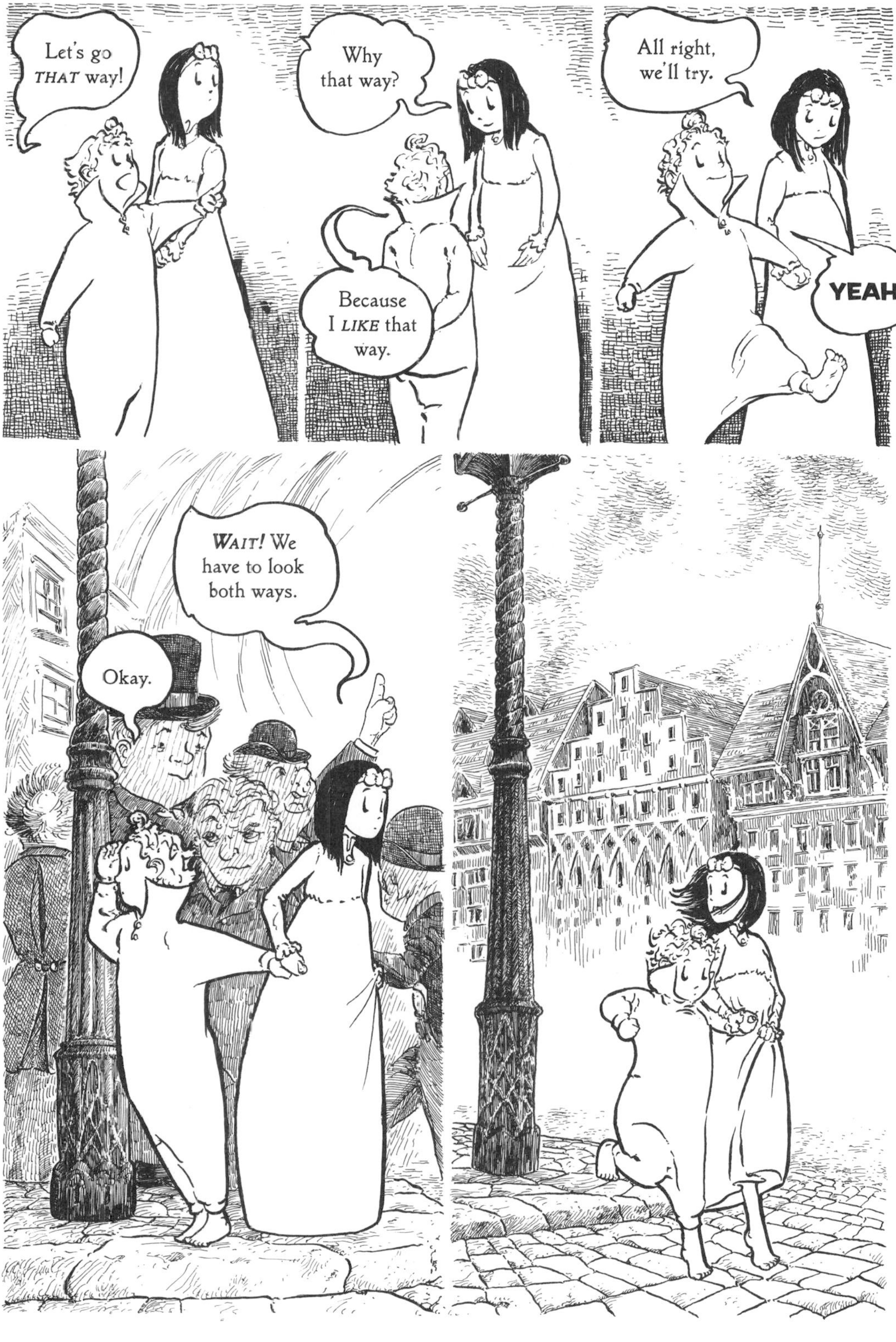
Let's go *THAT* way!
Why that way?
Because I *LIKE* that way.
All right, we'll try.
YEAH!
WAIT! We have to look both ways.
Okay.

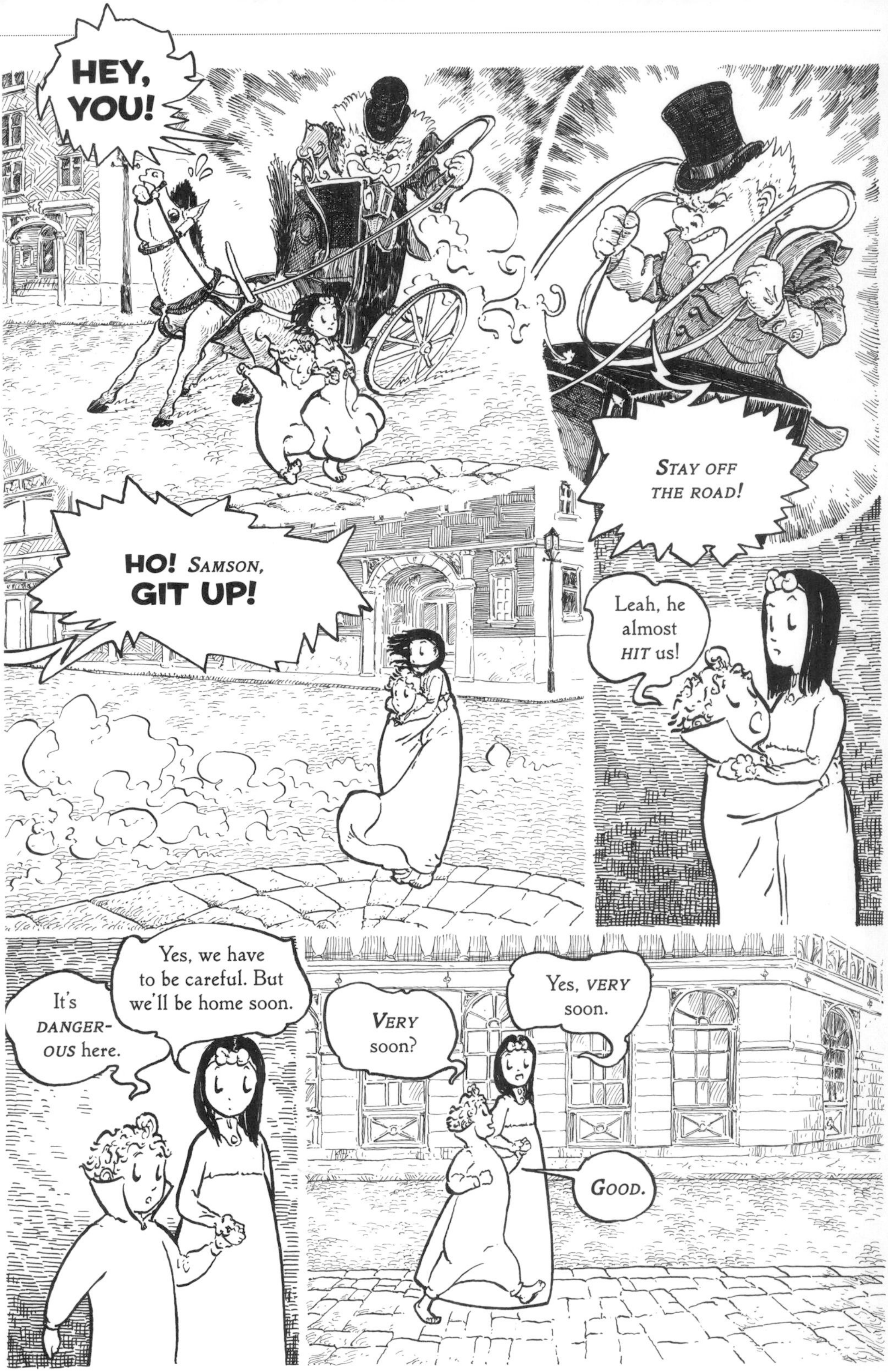
HEY, YOU!
STAY OFF THE ROAD!
HO! SAMSON, GIT UP!
Leah, he almost HIT us!
It's DANGER-OUS here.
Yes, we have to be careful. But we'll be home soon.
VERY soon?
Yes, VERY soon.
GOOD.

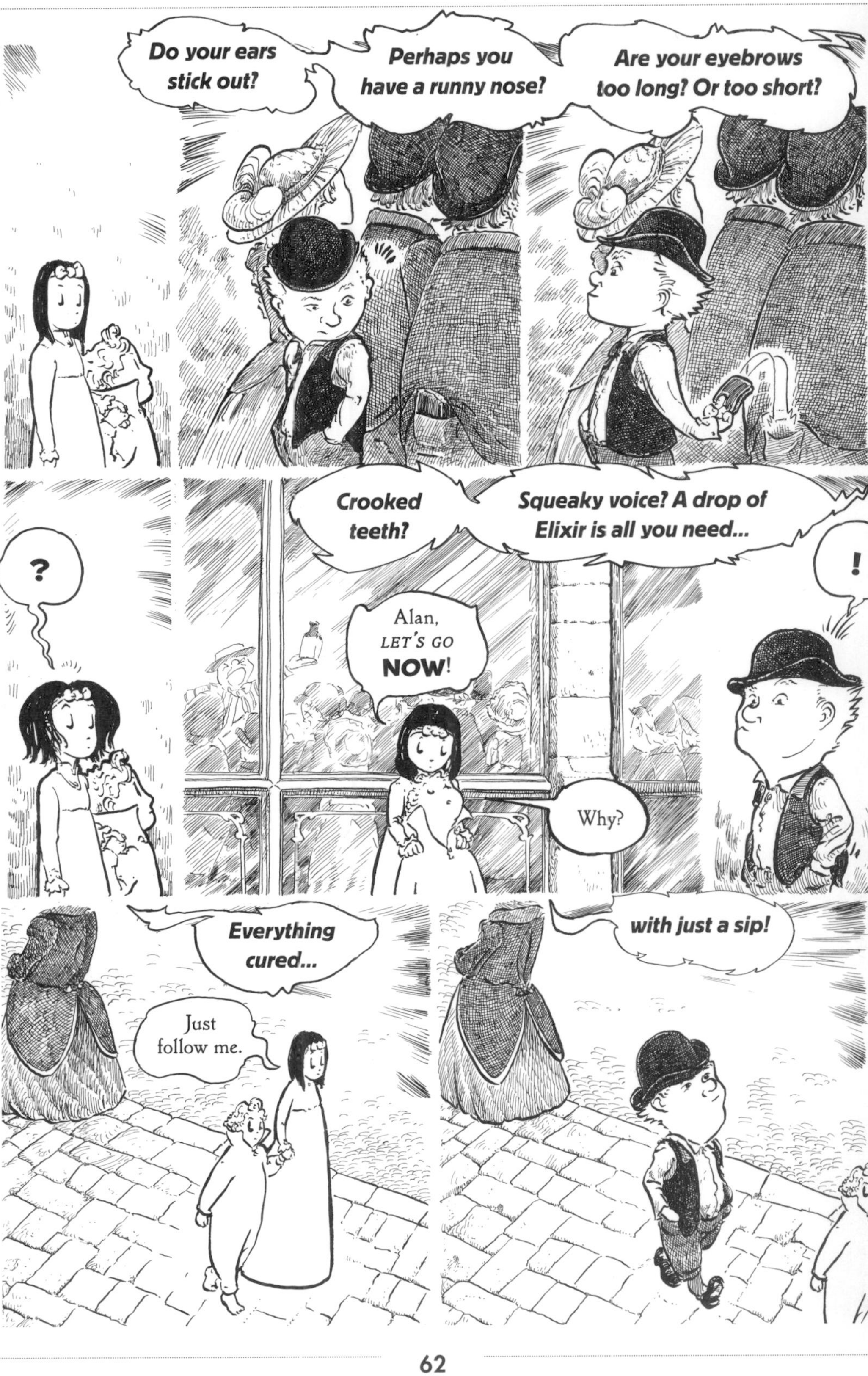

Do your ears stick out?
Perhaps you have a runny nose?
Are your eyebrows too long? Or too short?
?
Crooked teeth?
Squeaky voice? A drop of Elixir is all you need...
!
Alan, LET'S GO NOW!
Why?
Everything cured...
Just follow me.
with just a sip!

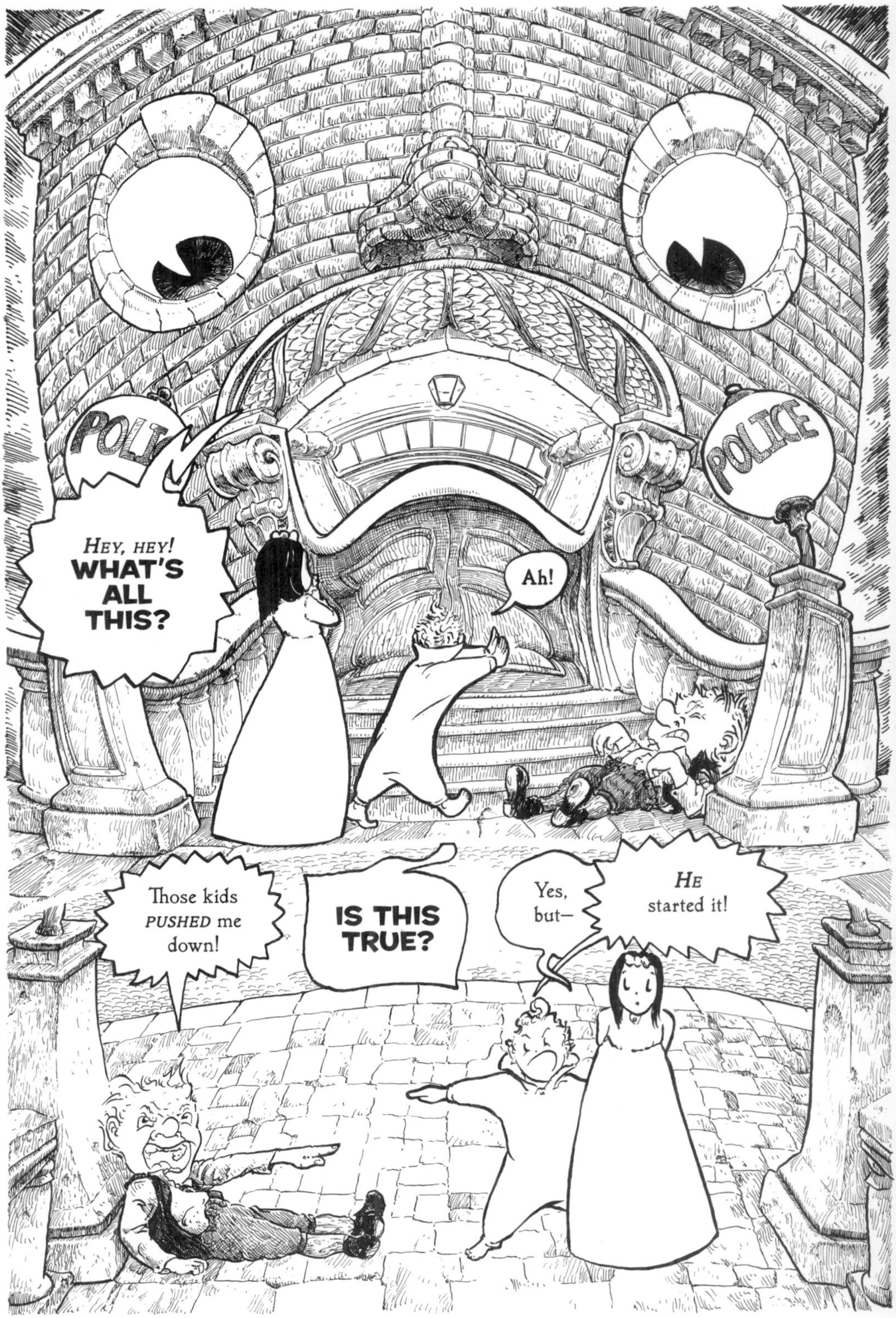
POLICE
POLICE
HEY, HEY! WHAT'S ALL THIS?
Ah!
Those kids PUSHED me down!
IS THIS TRUE?
Yes, but—
HE started it!

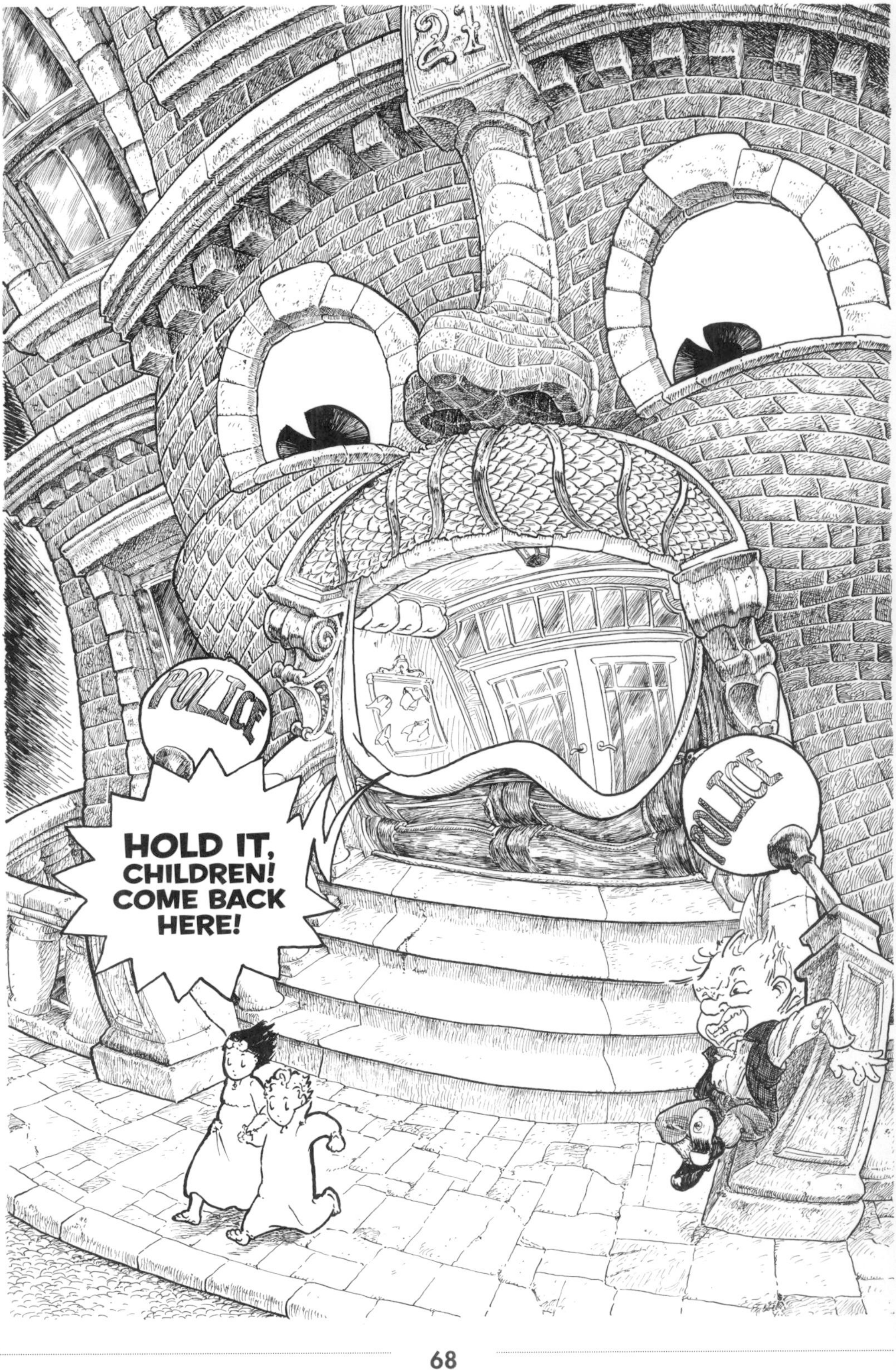
21
POLICE
POLICE
HOLD IT, CHILDREN! COME BACK HERE!

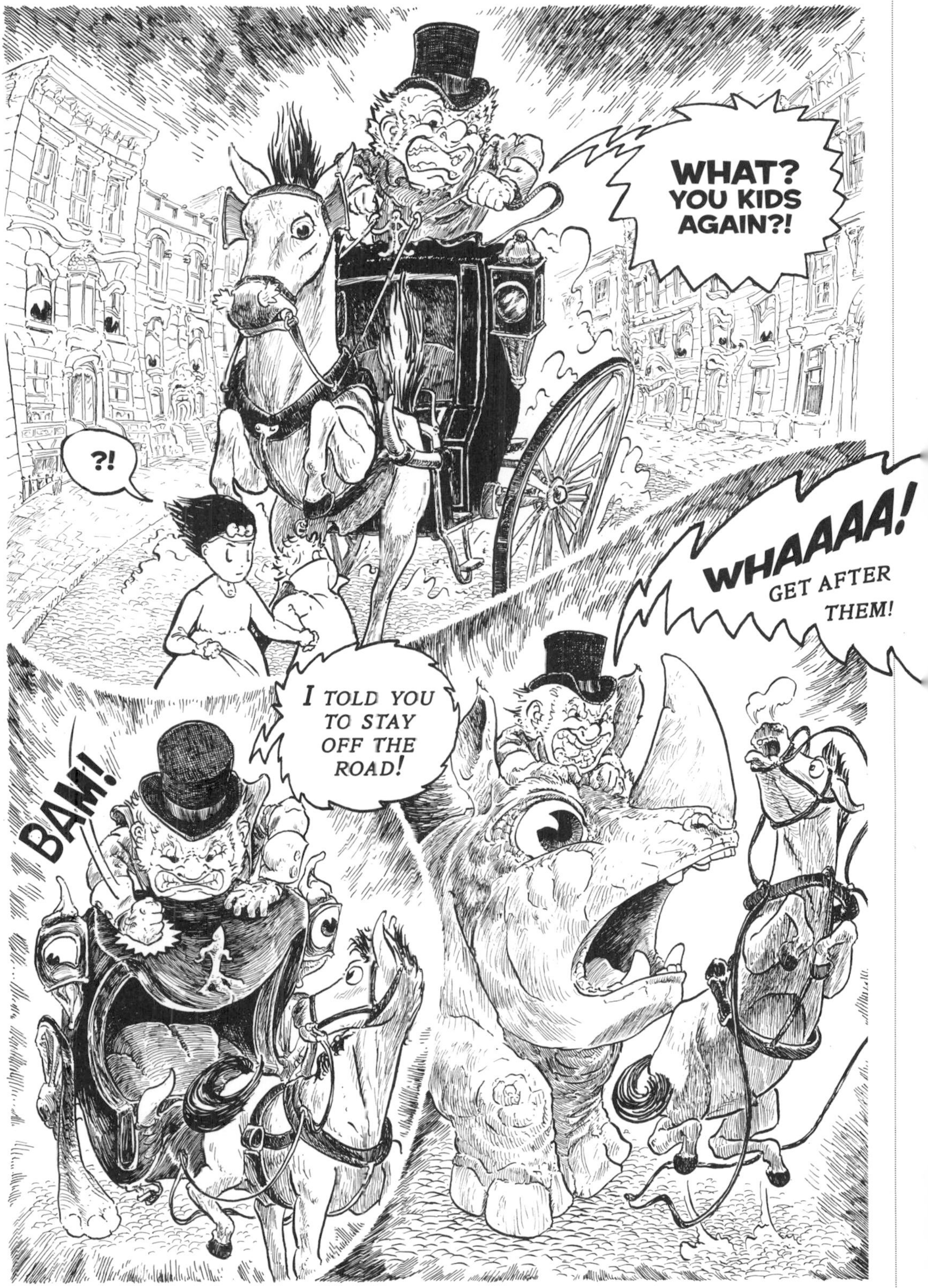
WHAT? YOU KIDS AGAIN?!
?!
WHAAAA! GET AFTER THEM!
I TOLD YOU TO STAY OFF THE ROAD!
BAM!

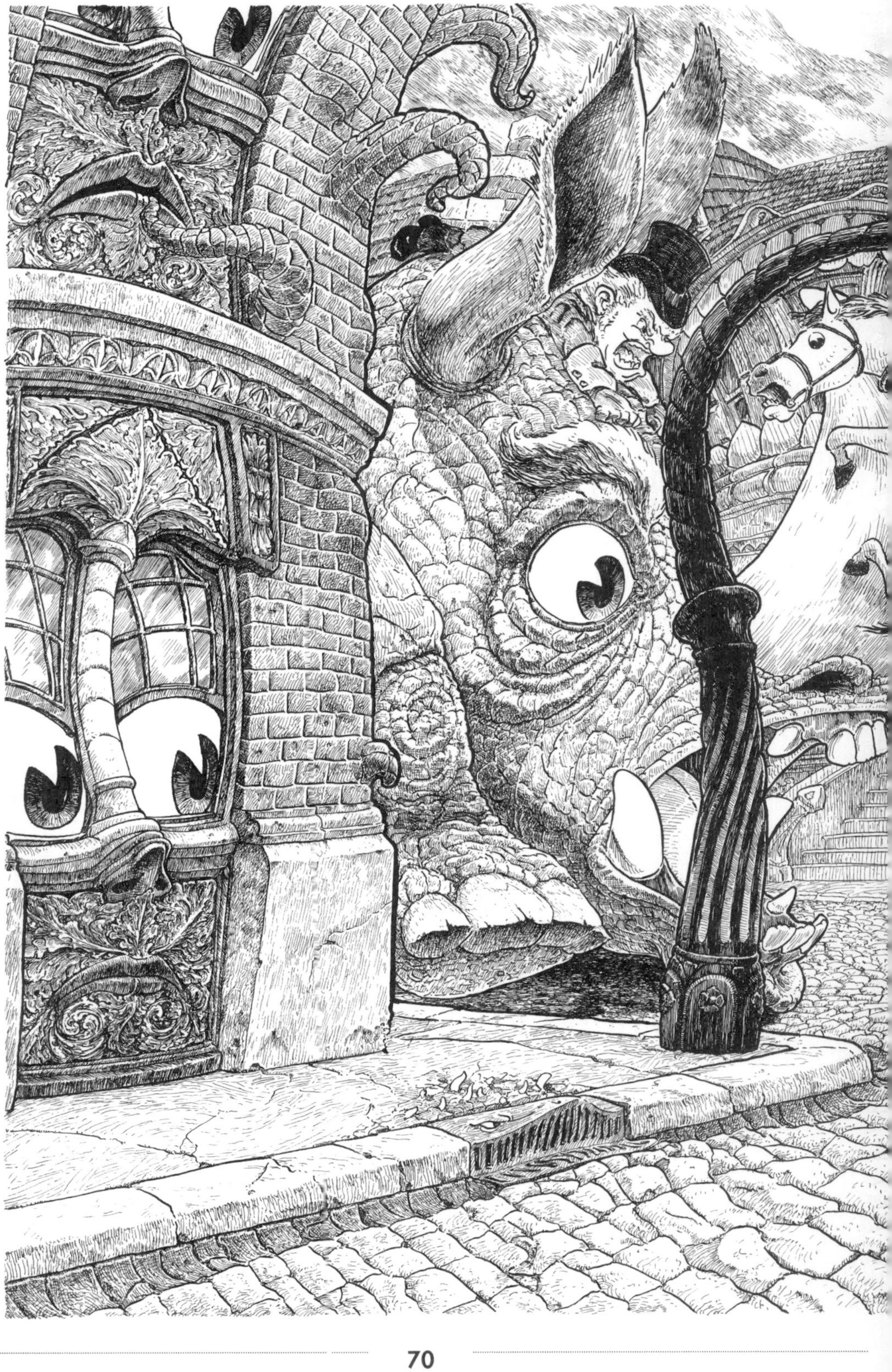

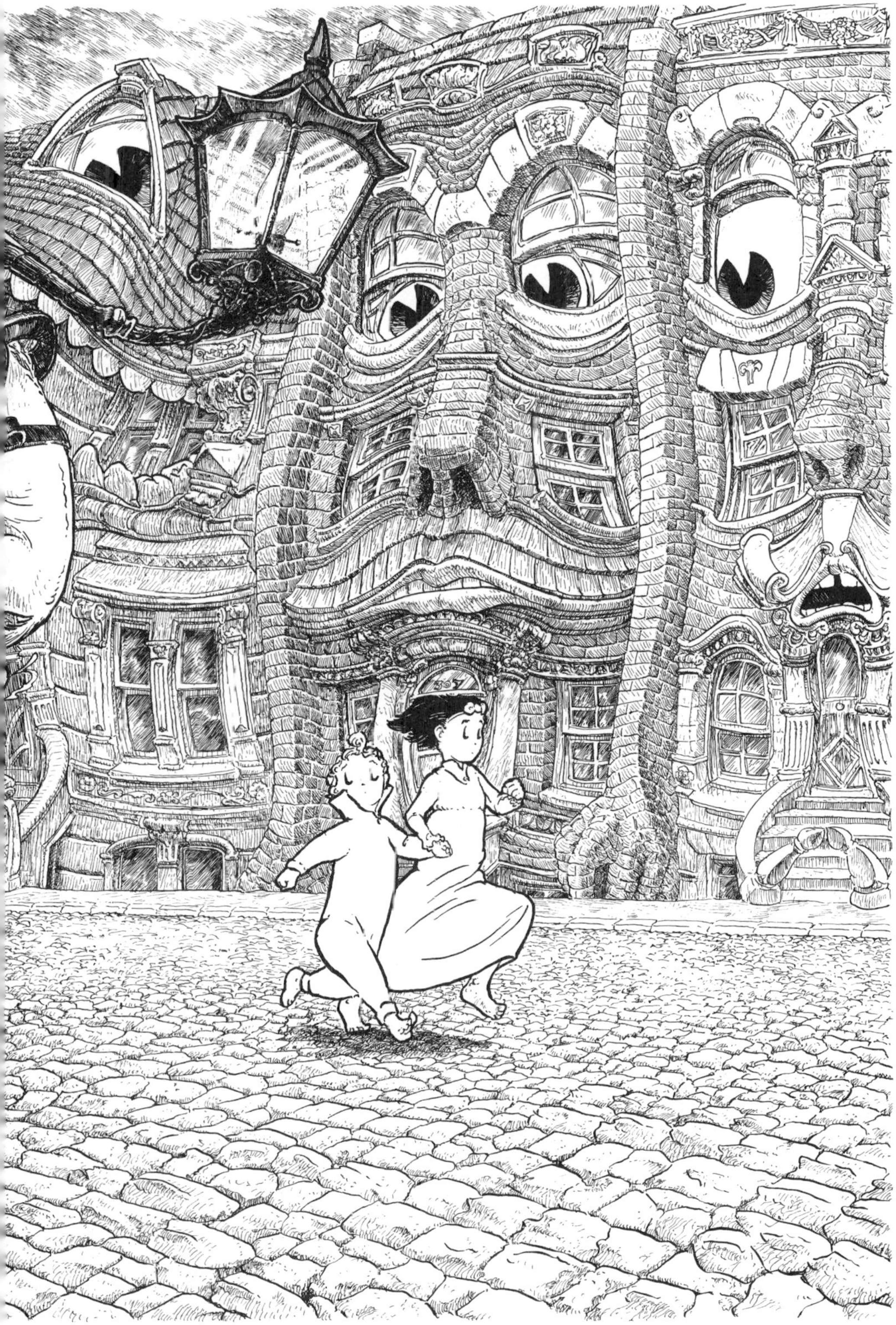

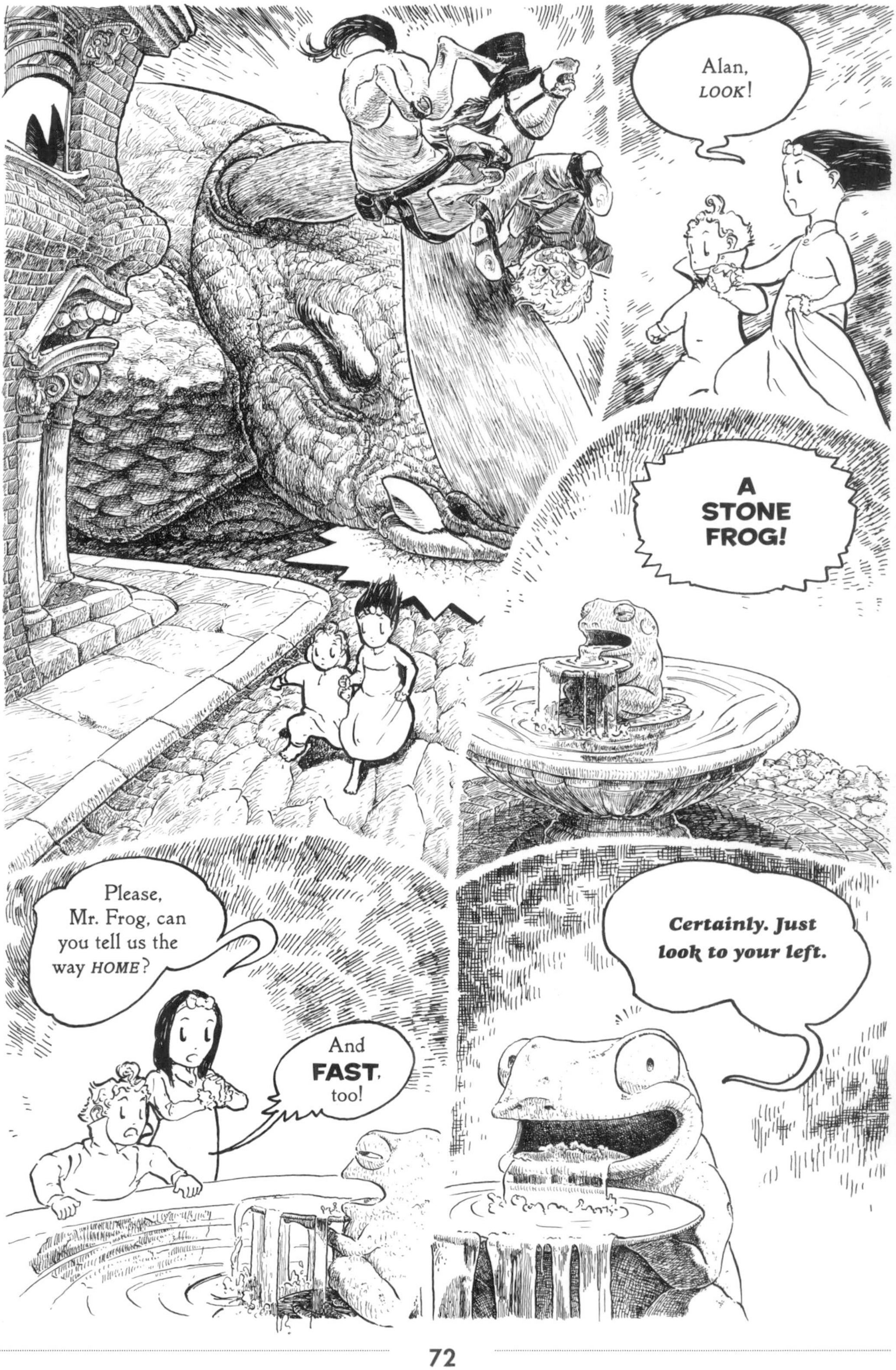
Alan, LOOK!
A STONE FROG!
Please, Mr. Frog, can you tell us the way HOME?
And FAST, too!
Certainly. Just look to your left.

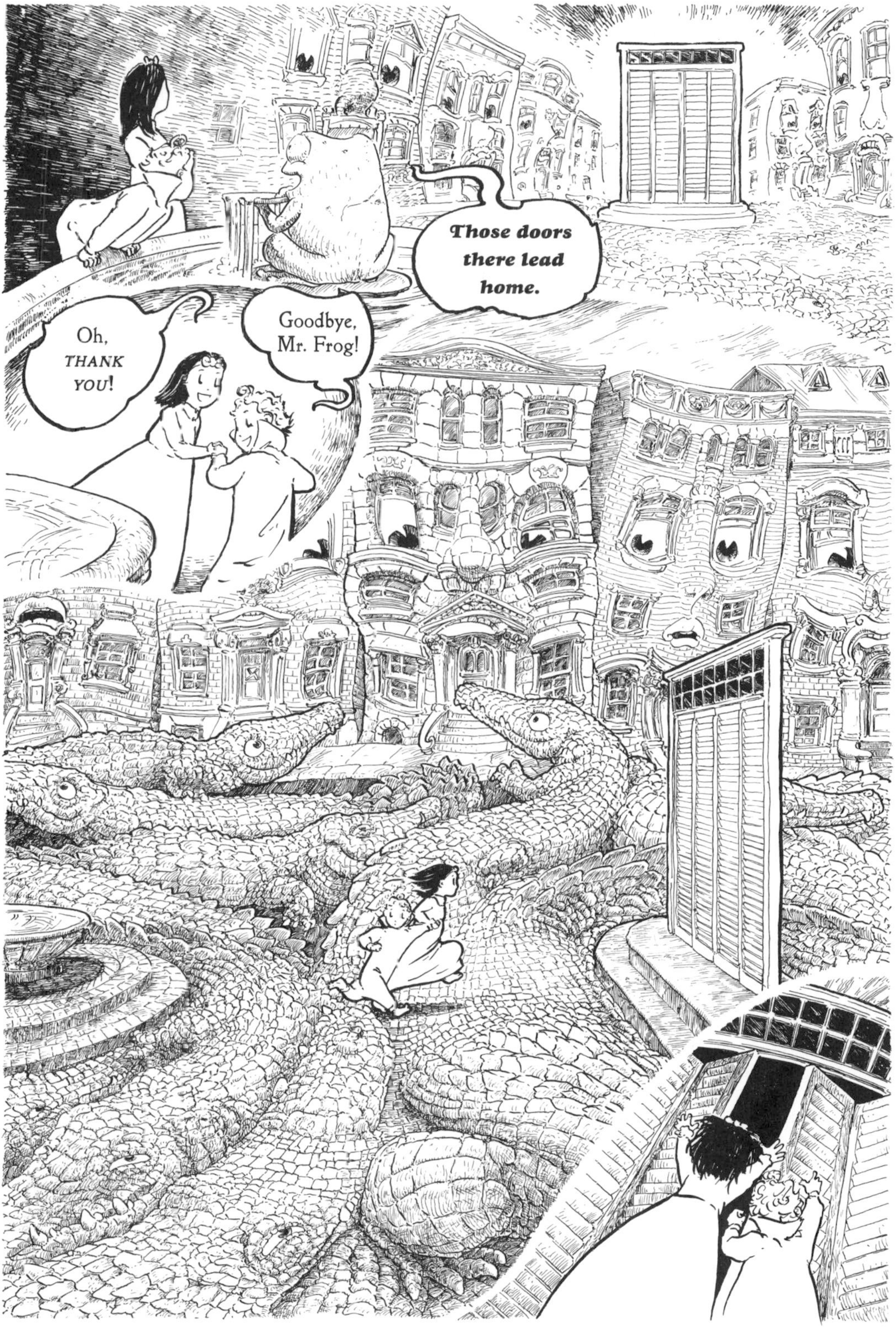
Those doors there lead home.
Oh, THANK YOU!
Goodbye, Mr. Frog!

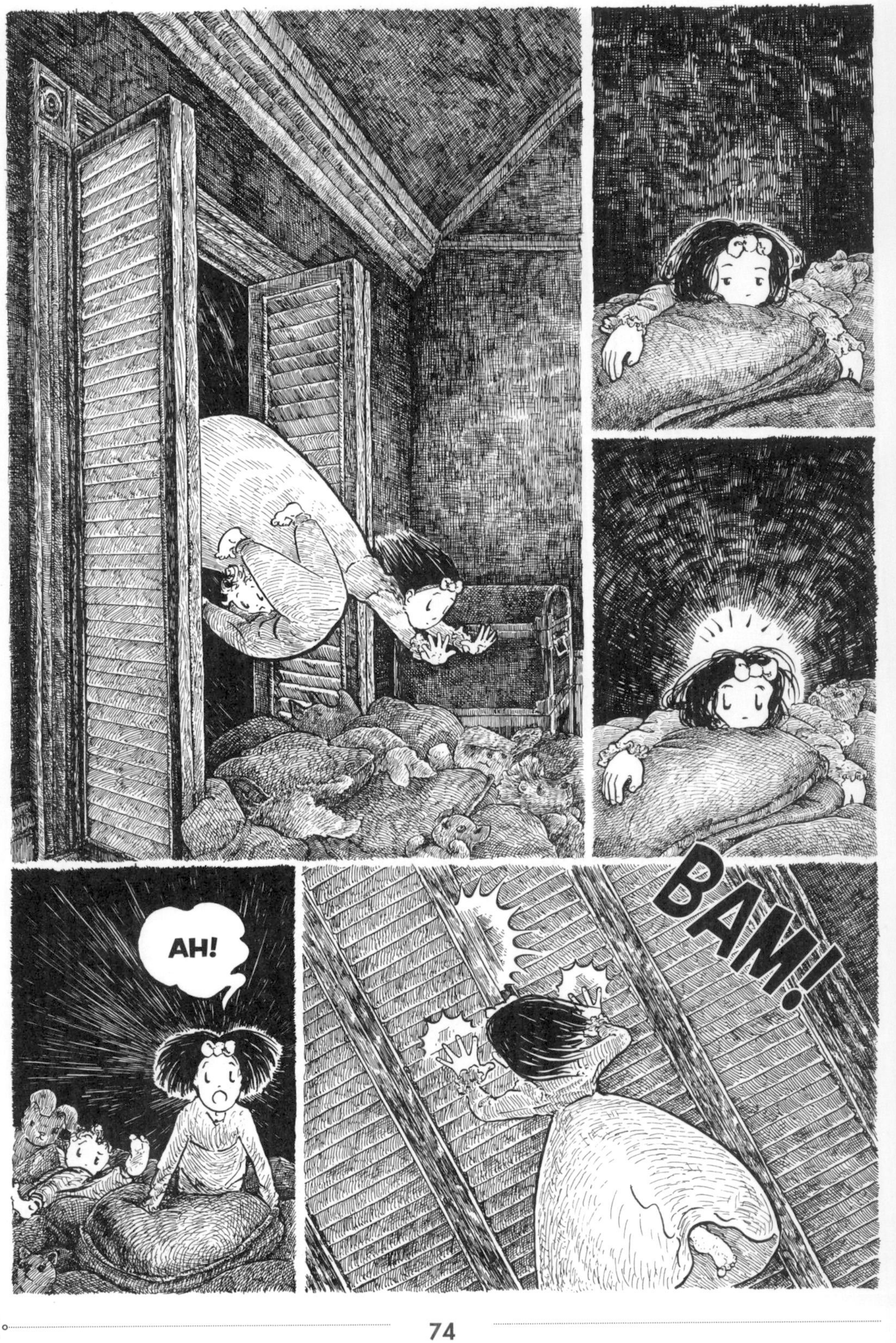
AH!
BAM!

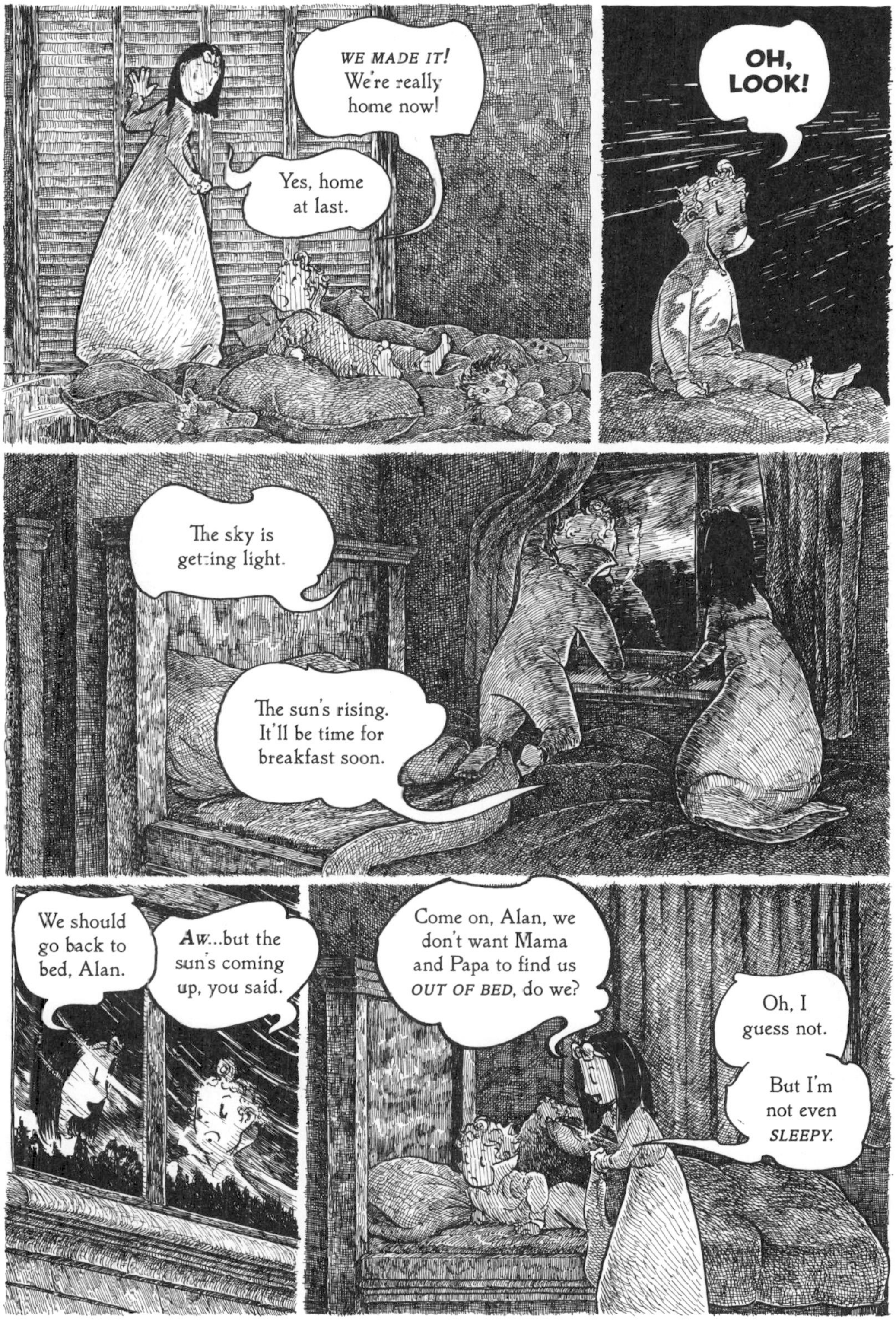
WE MADE IT! We're really home now!
Yes, home at last.
OH, LOOK!
The sky is getting light.
The sun's rising. It'll be time for breakfast soon.
We should go back to bed, Alan.
Aw...but the sun's coming up, you said.
Come on, Alan, we don't want Mama and Papa to find us OUT OF BED, do we?
Oh, I guess not.
But I'm not even SLEEPY.

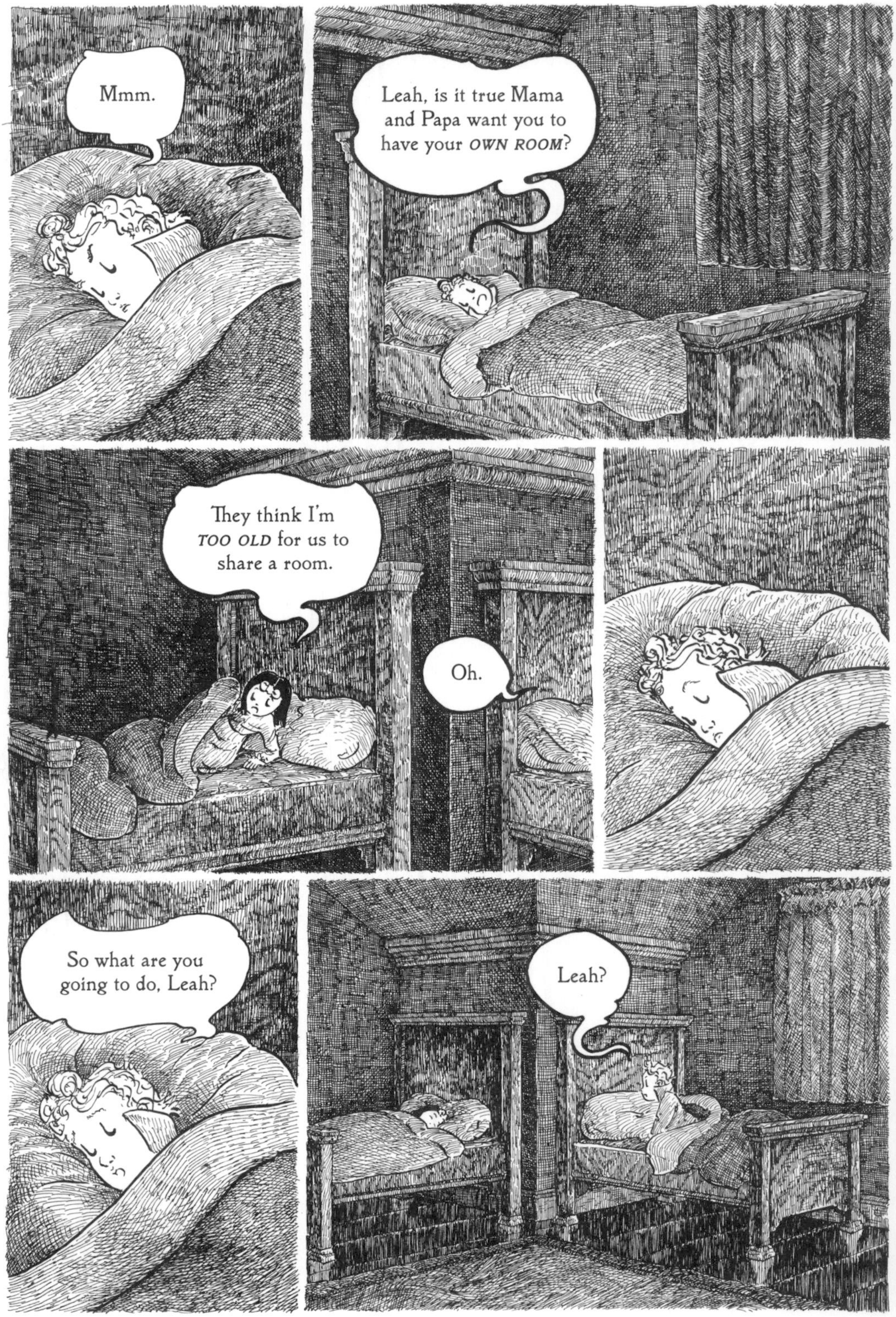
Mmm.
Leah, is it true Mama and Papa want you to have your *OWN ROOM*?
They think I'm *TOO OLD* for us to share a room.
Oh.
So what are you going to do, Leah?
Leah?

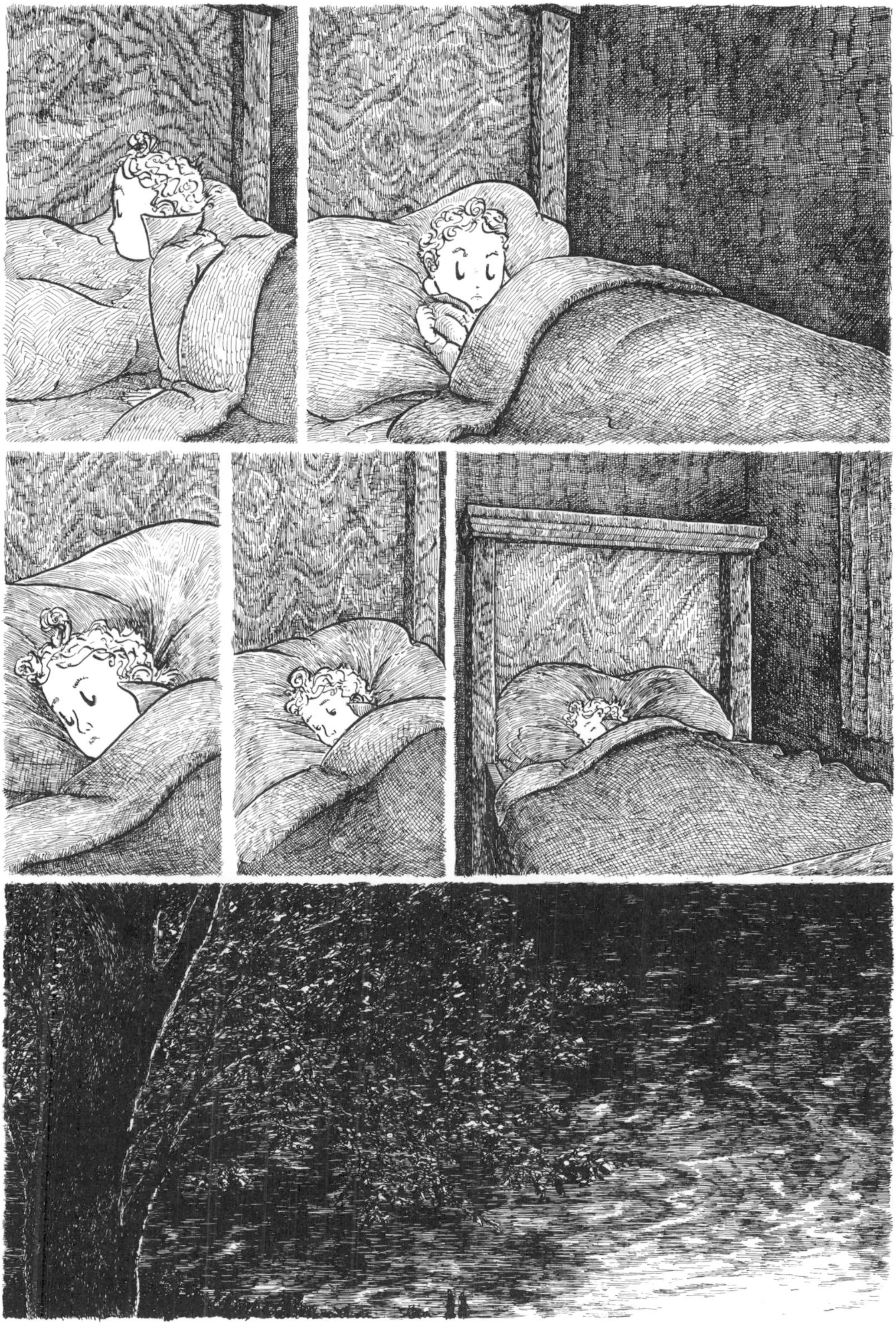

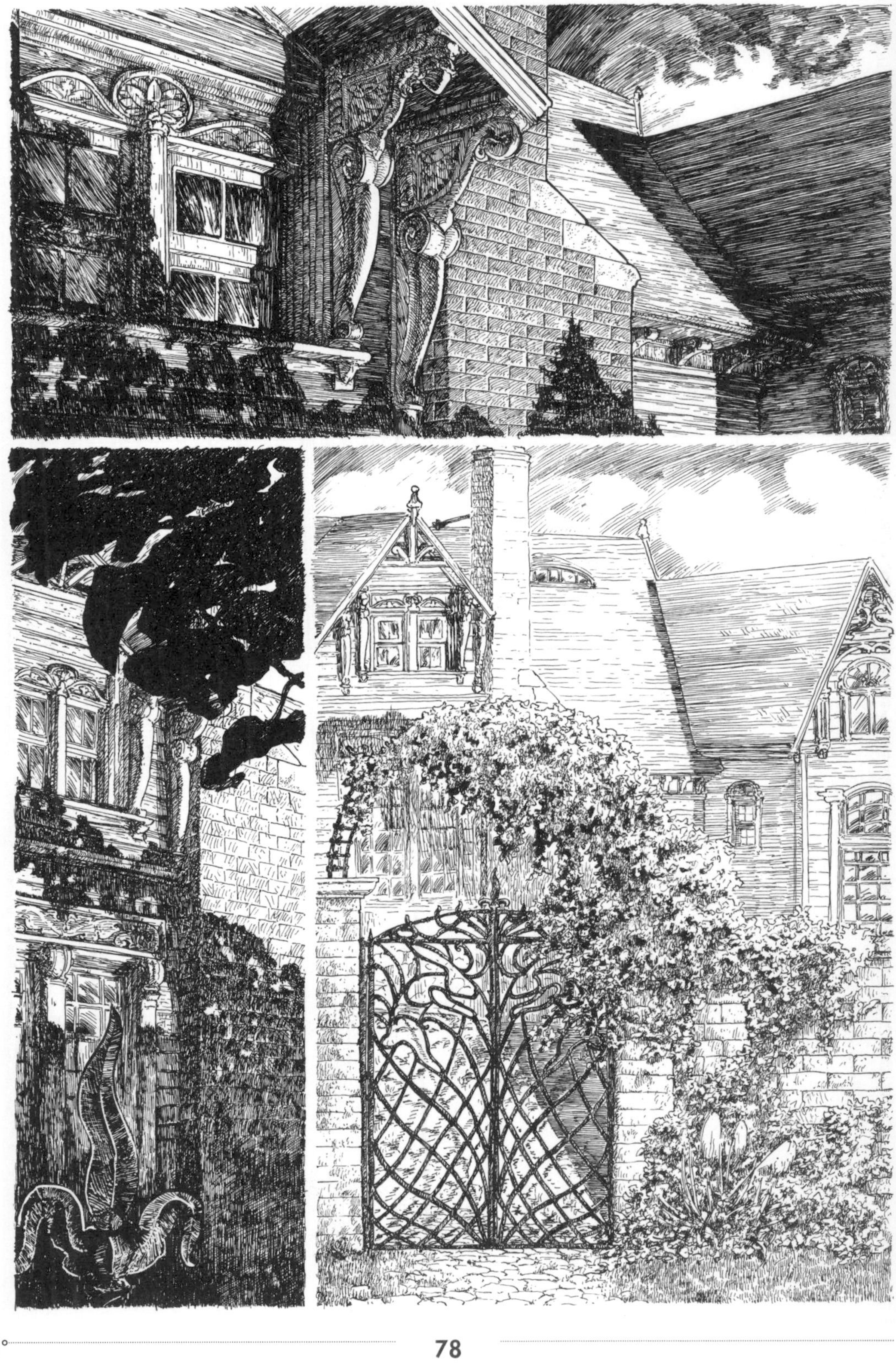

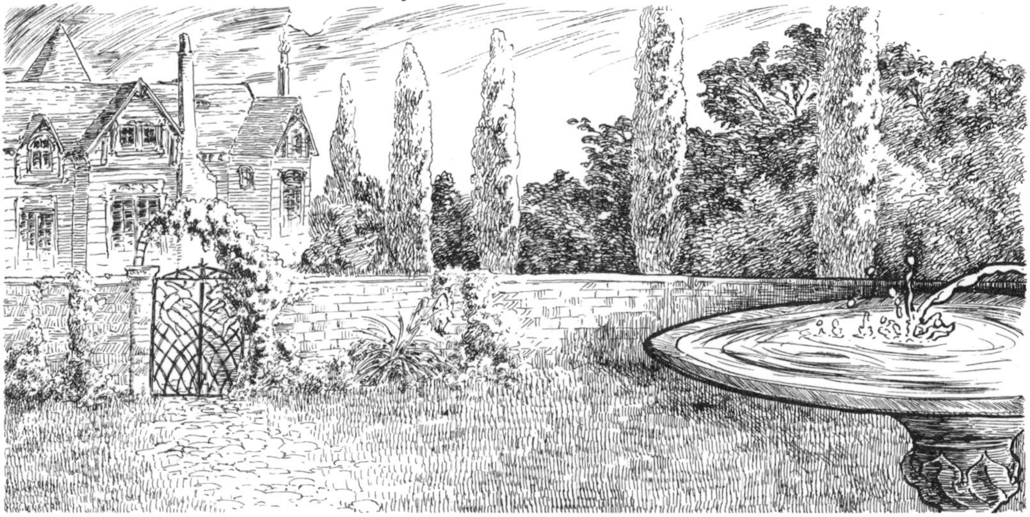

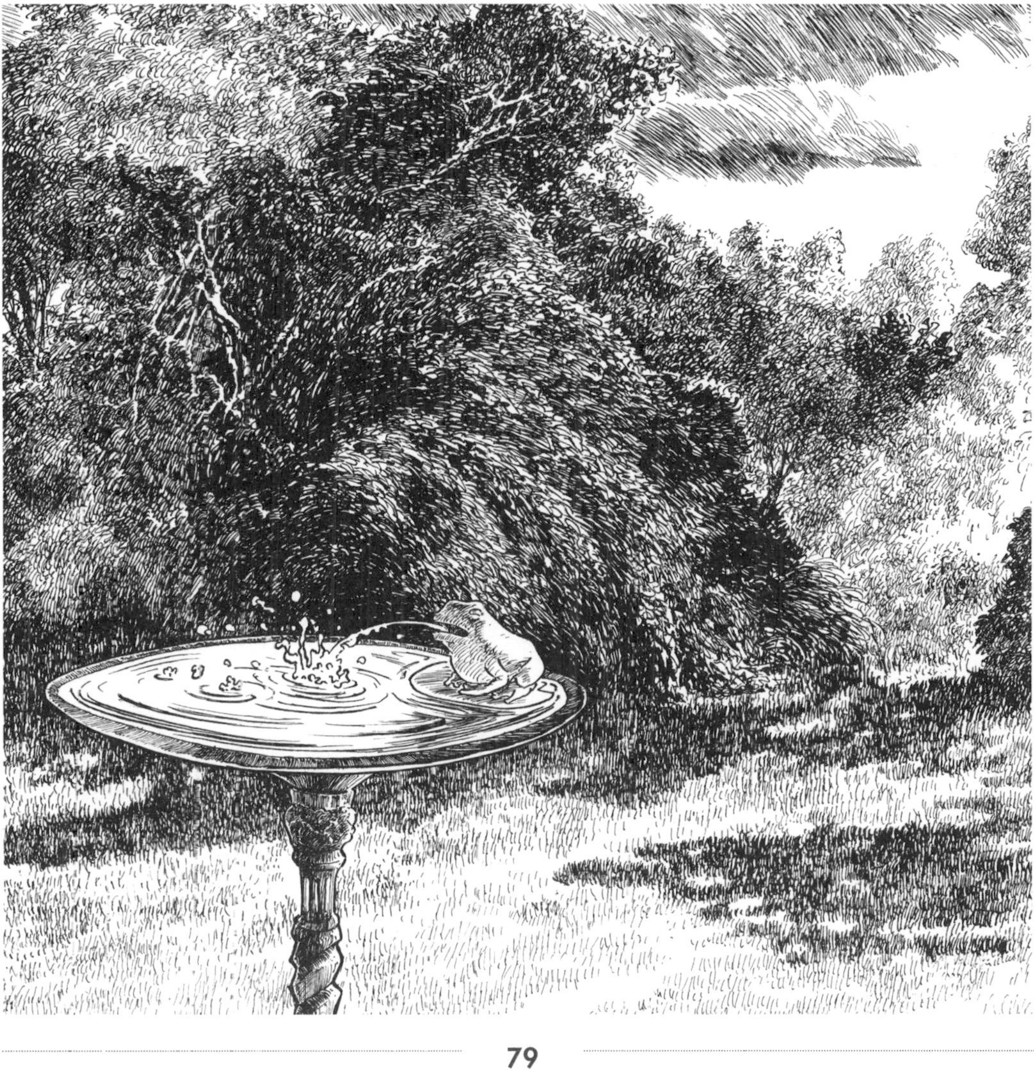

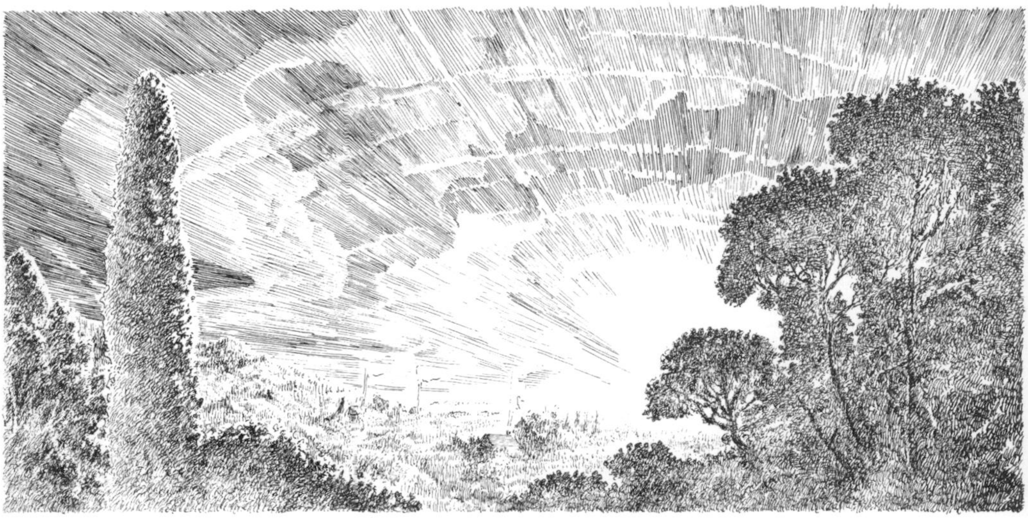

ABOUT THE AUTHOR

DAVID NYTRA has been drawing since he was old enough to hold a pencil. An artist who works in many media, including clay, wood, and animation, he lives in the small town of 100 Mile House in British Columbia, Canada. This is his first children's book. Though his own dreams are often unexciting and he's only a little bit allergic to bees, he loved books with many creatures in them as a child and he hopes he has put enough beasties in here to satisfy even the most demanding reader.

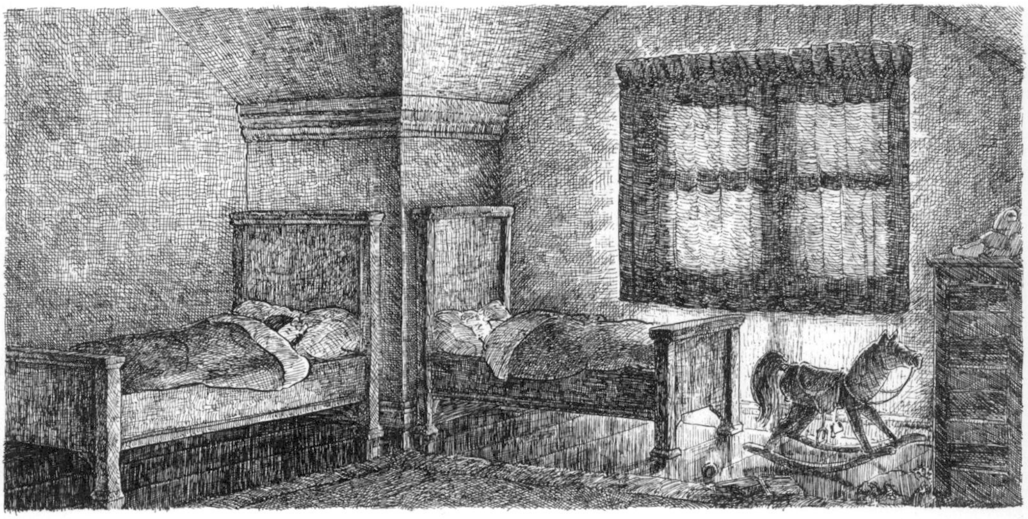